The RIGHT PLACE *at the* RIGHT TIME

a novel

MICHAELA CASEY

THE RIGHT PLACE AT THE RIGHT TIME
By Michaela Casey
Published by TouchPoint Press
www.touchpointpress.com

Softcover ISBN: 978-1-956851-69-4

Editor: Kelly Esparza and Sheri Williams
Cover Design: Sheri Williams
Cover image: Dorchester Market © Bill Forry

Library of Congress Control Number: On file

Printed in the United States of America.

To Lizzie Dwire and Grace Dwire Casey, who loved a good story, and to Bob O'Brien, who planted the seed for this one.

Prologue - A Year Later

A woman in early middle age stands at the front of a starkly lit and sparsely furnished basement classroom in the community center of an old Boston neighborhood long past its prime. The surrounding area was once dotted with pristine Victorians and lush pear orchards, but most of those are long gone, replaced by three-deckers, gas stations, and convenience stores.

Like the neighborhood, the woman herself is not considered attractive—by strangers, that is, if they consider her at all. Not homely, really, just . . . plain—small grayish eyes, pale complexion, dull brown hair pulled back in a careless ponytail. A generous few might envision that the right hairstyle with a few highlights, a little make-up (probably more than a little), and some toning, especially through the midriff, might get her, if not close to the mark, at least closer. People who know her, though, including the fifteen seated at desks before her, perceive nothing plain about her, no flaws to correct. They recognize that she has reached a higher mark of beauty, simply because they feel it whenever they are with her.

Smiling, she scans the faces of her students, who range from young to old and dark to light. However different they look, she has learned that they hold a common hope, the same hope her Irish grandparents had when they immigrated over a hundred years earlier—that after long and arduous journeys, they will find what eluded them in their native countries. She knows, too, that some of them will eventually leave this working-class neighborhood to "move up," as she did. But she likes to think that a few might choose, as she did, to move back. Today, though, she can tell from their eager faces and poised pencils that they have nothing on their minds but improving their English.

"Okay, whose turn is it to present the idiom of the day?" she asks them.

A young man wearing a vivid green Celtics t-shirt that is too big for his slight frame raises his hand.

"Take it away then, Miguel."

"Get started—right, Maggie?" Miguel replies.

"You've been reviewing. I love it."

With a proud smile, Miguel steps to the white board with his notebook and writes with a marker: *The right place at the right time.*

"Interesting choice," Maggie says.

"Is good?"

"Oh, yes. It's very good."

Miguel turns to his classmates.

"Okay, who can guess?"

Eyebrows furrow and lips purse, but the effort produces nothing but silence.

"I think maybe a sentence using the phrase might help them, Miguel."

Miguel nods and then copies from his notebook: *Sometimes you find what you need just by being in the right place at the right time.*

"So, who can know my idiom now?" he asks.

Brows furrow and lips purse again. This time, though, a soft, quavering voice arises.

"Maybe . . . don't be late for dinner?"

Maggie presses her lips together to suppress a smile and then says, "Well, that makes sense,

Yasmin, but there's a little more to it than that. Go ahead, Miguel, and tell them."

Miguel reads: *To be somewhere just when a good opportunity happens.*

"Like we are here in class?" an older man in the back row asks.

"You're in the ballpark, Tran," Maggie replies.

"A little close, yes?" says Tran.

"Ah, you've been reviewing, too. Yes, you are close. The difference is that you come to class because you *know* there will be an opportunity. Miguel's idiom means that you don't really know that a good thing is going to happen when you go to the place."

"Is like, then, good fortune?" an eager-eyed girl suggests.

"That's it, Ana. Good fortune, especially when you're not expecting it."

As the rest of the class jots down the definition, Miguel turns to Maggie and asks, "This really happens in America?"

Maggie takes a slow breath, as if someone has just handed her a fresh-baked cinnamon roll.

"Oh . . . yes, Miguel," she answers. "Sometimes it really happens."

1 - A Wild Ride

In her designer kitchen with its top-of-the-line appliances and custom-made cabinetry, in her "gracious" (according to the real estate agent) Victorian in a "fabulous" (again, the agent), Chestnut Hill neighborhood, Maggie Dodge was serving up one of the soups she had learned to make on a cheap stove in her family's run-of the-mill three-decker apartment, crammed among scores of look-alikes on a narrow side street within earshot of the Southeast Expressway and the Red Line transit tracks in dingy old Dorchester.

It was the same street where she and her husband, Wilford "Wil" Dodge, then a rookie sports reporter for the *Boston Globe*, had an almost identical apartment for the first few years of their marriage. Maggie once told Wil that the name of the street, Bay View, never made sense to her because you couldn't see the water from anywhere on it. A few days later, he brought her up to the roof with a pair of high-power binoculars to show her that he had indeed sighted Dorchester Bay. The sliver of blue that Maggie vaguely perceived didn't change her mind, but Wil was smiling the way he always did when he thought he had proven himself right, and she didn't want to spoil his moment.

"Wow," she said. "Who knew?"

Wil's embrace of the neighborhood—it had been his idea to live there—surprised her. His family had offered to help them buy a house near theirs in suburban Marblehead, where you didn't need to strain your eyes or your imagination to see the ocean, so she figured that's where they would go. Wil, though, insisted that the neighborhood in "Dot," as he loved to call it, was much more "authentic." Maggie wasn't sure what was so authentic about the jumble of mom-and-pops, liquor stores, auto-glass shops, and laundromats that surrounded them, but she was relieved not to have to live near her in-laws, Prescott and Virginia Dodge. It wasn't that they were unfriendly to her; in fact, every visit to their home began and ended with hugs, which took Maggie a while to get used to because her family was non-hugging Irish.

The Dodges even urged her to call them "Press" and "Ginger," insisting that "Mr." and "Mrs." were too formal now that she was "family." Maggie did greet them with their first names once, but it felt too weird, kind of like calling the Queen of England and her husband "Lizzie" and "Phil." She preferred being formal with her in-laws, maybe because she really couldn't see them as family any more than she could the royal couple. Of course, this left her with nothing to call them. At first, she worried that they would chide her about never addressing them by name, but almost ten years into her marriage, neither they nor Wil had ever said anything about it.

No matter how welcoming the Dodges were to her, though, Maggie always felt like their Eliza Doolittle. Mr. Dodge was certainly well meaning with his jovial insistence that she learn how to sail or that she let him help her with her tennis game, but the former offer filled Maggie with dread because she had not stepped foot on a boat since vomiting all over Sister Mary Lucille's shoes on the Nantasket Beach ferry during her eighth-grade class trip, and the latter with shame that she had no tennis game *to* improve. Mrs. Dodge's suggestions for Maggie's improvement were more aesthetic—make-up artists, dressmakers, and hair stylists—all delivered with a benign but pitying smile.

Maggie knew that living in Dorchester would at least distance her from the Dodges' solicitousness. Like many suburbanites she had met, her in-laws were sure to be scared off by the area's reputation for street crime, making it unlikely that they would drop in to whisk her off to a tennis court or a beauty salon. Maggie had no intention of telling them that most of the shootings and stabbings they saw on TV news occurred miles away from Bay View Street, and she could count on Wil not to break her cover, because he enjoyed his parents' misperception that he lived among "hoodlums."

Wil's fascination with Dorchester faded, though, a few years later. By that time, he had gotten his own column, which became syndicated, landed some commentary work on TV, and co-authored a book with a retired big-league umpire about his legendary run-ins with irate ballplayers and managers, *What I Say Goes*, which became a national bestseller. Wil explained to Maggie that at this level of his career, a suburban Chestnut Hill address would be more "appropriate" for them. The house they ended up choosing—well, that Wil chose and Maggie went along with—was just what anybody else on Bay View Street would buy if just one of the twenty lottery tickets they bought every week would pay off, but after all these years, it still looked and felt to Maggie like somebody else's house—Ginger Dodge's.

Maggie blamed herself for this predicament because the first time her mother-in-law popped in with "a few décor visions," it was abundantly clear that Maggie had none of her own. All she saw when she looked around the house were ten oversized, empty rooms that she could not imagine filling, much less "stylizing." Wallpaper books, fabric and paint swatches, and furniture stores made her panicky—way too many choices! And so, like a non-swimmer who has fallen into the deep end of a pool, Maggie accepted each of Mrs. Dodge's ideas as if it were a life preserver. The result was a house fit for a magazine—and, in fact, Mrs. Dodge had used her connections to score a spread in *Suburban Elegance*—but also one that Maggie was still no more comfortable in than she would be at Buckingham Palace.

Making soup, though, always made her feel at home, and today she ladled it (split pea, secret ingredient: crème sherry) into a bowl that she placed before a slight, gray-haired woman at the kitchen table. The recipient brought a brimming spoonful to her mouth, swallowed, and smiled. Her face was not as dazzling as it was in photos Maggie had seen of the woman in the youthful bloom of her beauty, when her flawless complexion was framed by lustrous brown hair, but that smile had never lost its radiance, and it lifted Maggie's spirits whenever she saw it.

"I do love soup," the woman said, scooping up another taste. She suspended this one, though, halfway to its destination and looked over at Maggie with curiosity etched between her fading eyebrows.

"Does *your* mother like soup?" she asked.

Maggie's own eyebrows rose, despite her conviction that by now questions like this should be unremarkable. Granted, the woman asking it was her own mother, Edna McDonough, but over a year into Edna's cognitive slide, shouldn't Maggie be able to accept its manifestations as the new normal, or as Edna would describe it if she could, "God's will?" Of course, she should!

Perversely, though, they intrigued Maggie like plot twists in a novel. This was not to say that she enjoyed Edna's journey into dementia, an unkind word that made her wince whenever the geriatrician said it. She had always considered herself a good daughter—and now a devoted caregiver—and was profoundly saddened by Edna's decline. And yet, Maggie could not deny a growing, and she feared, disrespectful fascination with it: likening her own mother to a page turner! Her rational mind argued that she would have to be senile (another disdainful word) herself not to be fascinated by a transformation of such dramatic proportions.

After all, this woman, who was now as opinionated and aggressive as a newborn lamb, had

once been the indomitable leader of the Boston Clerical Workers Union and a wily political operative, who mastered the use of local media outlets to arouse public sympathy for the membership's objectives. (She called them "needs.) A classic example of her tactics was her push for a new clause in the municipal contract that would include eye exams and eyeglasses for all office workers and their families, a proposal to which Mayor Slavin publicly replied, "Really? What else? Red Sox season tickets?"

Emboldened by his dismissiveness, Edna organized an outdoor rally in treeless City Hall Plaza, where, surrounded by her squinting colleagues and their squinting children—

she had scheduled the event for noontime on a cloudless July day—and by a phalanx of reporters, eager for one of her delectable sound bites, she looked into the cameras and declared, "Mr. Mayor, *eye* care means *you* care about your people!"

Hizzoner caved the next day.

Edna was no less a force on the home front, enabled by a peace-loving husband, Philip "Sweety" McDonough, and Maggie herself, who took after him, both of whom saw the path of least resistance as preferable to the path of the maternal *Sturm und Drang* that would result from opposing her.

For Maggie, though, conflict avoidance was only one reason for her compliance. The other, and perhaps stronger, motivation was decision avoidance. Perhaps this was the result of the strictures of parochial schooling or perhaps the reason that she took to them so naturally. During her years at Saint Aloysius Grammar School and Monsignor Farrell High, every aspect of life was scripted: what to wear and what to believe, when to speak up (rarely) and when to listen (always), how to memorize and how to pray. Reared on the Baltimore Catechism, papal edicts, the Ten Commandments of God, the five commandments of the Catholic Church, and the rules of deportment set by the Sisters of Piety, all Maggie had to decide was whether to follow them, or, as many of her classmates did, find every possible way to get around them because they were "wicked stupid." Again, Maggie followed her father's pragmatic lead and simply conformed to the prevailing power.

At home, this was held by Edna, whose pronouncements—Sweety called them "Mum's Way"—held sway like . . . well, like a nun's. When Maggie had to make up her mind—say, about an opening sentence for an essay or a birthday present for a friend—she struggled inordinately out of fear that she would make the wrong choice, because after all, there had to be a right way and a wrong way to do everything. She always marveled at the swiftness of her mother's decision-making process, which seemed less like a process and more like a high-speed reflex. Thus, it was decreed that Maggie would take Latin, not French; cross-country, not soccer; and painting, not photography. Similarly, she was directed to volunteer at the Maryknoll nursing home, to keep her hair its natural color, and to avoid Billy Hallahan no matter how cute he was. Maggie chafed at some of these edicts—Billy Hallahan was *very* cute—but generally she was relieved by them because they spared her hours, if not days, of indecision that would have resulted in a wimpy flip-of-a-coin, followed by intensive second-guessing.

But even though Edna's mental metamorphosis from a race car to a buggy would enthrall any rational person, Maggie's Irish Catholic conscience still made her feel guilty. To her credit, though, or perhaps to the credit of a Germanic strain in Edna's lineage, logic fought back, like an outclassed boxer who keeps staggering to his feet only to be knocked down again.

In the early stages of Edna's transformation, Maggie would have responded to the soup question by trying to drag her mother back to reality: "*You're* my mother! You're the one who taught me to make soup! Remember chicken vegetable with tapioca? And cream of mushroom with honey mustard? And corn chowder with Irish whiskey? 'Soup needs a secret.' That's what you used to say! *Remember*?"

Before long, though, Maggie saw that Edna was on a one-way journey to a different reality and that trying to reverse it only sped it up. Maggie was initially disoriented by the shift, almost as if the law of gravity had been repealed, but over time she adjusted to floating—got to like it even—by simply doing what she had always done: going along with whatever her mother said.

And so, she now replied, "Oh, yes, my mother loves soup."

At this, the wrinkles on Edna's forehead deepened, and Maggie suspected that she was puzzling over the identity of this fellow soup lover. But within seconds, her smile returned, and she resumed eating. Maggie's pulse quickened in anticipation of the next leg of the journey.

"I used to know your mother," Edna said in her old no-doubt-about-it tone.

"Oh, really?" Maggie replied, as uneagerly as she could.

"We used to work together in . . . in the big building where you tap the keys with your fingers."

"City Hall," Maggie offered.

"No," Edna scoffed, "right over there," and she pointed toward the window and the garden shed in the backyard. Nodding reminiscently, she sipped more soup and continued. "She was a good spud, your mother. Stood up to the bosses for us, y'know. Everybody liked her. 'Specially the fellas."

This time Maggie made no attempt to mask her curiosity.

"Tell me about it," she said, pulling up a chair.

"Don't you remember Friday nights after work? The whole gang would go over . . . over there." She pointed toward another window and the house next door. "The place with all the bottles. Oh, she was the bubbles in the beer, she was. Always jokin' and laughin' and flouncin' around. A'course, the little brown glasses helped. She could really knock them back."

She surveyed the room furtively, then leaned toward Maggie and whispered, "And I'll tell ya another thing. Come closing—*she never left alone.*"

Maggie's mouth opened, but no words came out. Edna, however, was on a roll.

"Had to have her *physical activity,*" she said. "You know—the kind that makes the bed squeak." A naughty little wink, a teasing pause for soup, and the clincher, "Except they always did it in a car."

Edna's eyes closed dreamily, her cheeks erupting in a passionate glow, her smile radiating satisfaction way beyond anything pea soup could arouse. Any thought Maggie might have entertained that Edna had been talking about someone else evaporated in the heat of this blatant back-seat-of-a-Buick bliss.

From the depths of this reverie, Edna's voice reemerged. "Yup. She was a wild ride."

"Wild . . . ride?" Maggie sputtered.

"Well, that's what all the fellas told her," Edna proclaimed, cocking her head. In the next instant, though, she frowned.

"Funny, though," she said in a subdued tone, "I can't remember her name."

"Edna," Maggie replied blankly.

"Edna? Ha! I thought she was a *good* girl."

2 - Sweety Dream

From the doorway of the living room, Maggie watched her mother pretending to say the rosary. Her fingers were massaging the beads but making no progress through the decades, and her lips were not moving the way they did when she used to really pray. Her eyes, instead of being half shut, were wandering around the room, as if searching for a clue as to her whereabouts.

When they stumbled upon Maggie, Edna exclaimed, "Well, hello, dearie!" Her joyful, what-a surprise-to-see-you-here tone made Maggie smile. Her mother might have forgotten who she was and that they were together just a few minutes earlier, but at least she was happy to see her.

"Is Robby home from school yet?" Edna asked. Not waiting for an answer, she continued. "Poor little kid. How did he get that way?"

She swayed back and forth in her plush rocker-recliner, propelled by a gentle, rhythmic two-step. Nearby was an identical chair that Maggie's seven-year-old son, Robby, would later occupy, as content as his grandmother to rock the afternoon away fingering rosary beads.

"No, Mum. Wil's picking him up at school and taking him to the gym today," Maggie said.

Before she could give her usual answer to the second question, "Nobody knows, Mum. It's just the way God made him," Edna asked, "Is Robby home from school yet? I hope he gets here in time to see Mutti and Rosamund. They're coming over today, you know. Have they called?"

"Um . . . no," Maggie said of her long-deceased grandmother and great-aunt. "I think they're resting."

"Oh, that's good. They need it. Is Robby home from school yet?"

Maggie settled into the empty rocker, picked up her mother's rhythm, and tried to channel some positive energy because she had read in Oprah's magazine that this can be a great help in dealing with life's challenges. Toward this end, she imagined that the place her mother was heading was something like the one Robby already inhabited—a place where there was no boredom, just comforting routines; no frustration, just passive acceptance; no loneliness, just natural solitude—kind of a cross between a spiritual retreat and a wellness resort. Thinking about it, she yawned.

Maggie's take on her son's condition had not always been so upbeat, especially when it was first diagnosed. When Robby was three years old, the specialist their pediatrician had sent them to for an evaluation described his findings in scary terms like "perseverative behaviors," "expressive language deficit," and "affective passivity," all pointing to a "generalized organic disorder." He had made it all sound so *bad*, as if Robby were defective merchandise. Trained by the nuns to defer to authority and blame herself, Maggie did just that and was cast into a purgatory of hopelessness and guilt. She wasn't surprised that Wil refused to go there.

"I'm not going to listen to a doctor with such a loser mentality," he told her. "Okay, Robby's down, but he's not out. What he needs—and I've been reading up on this, so I know—is high-quality intervention at a residential treatment center. I found an excellent one in the Berkshires. If he's ever going to get into the game, it'll be at a place like that."

Maggie sat and listened to him. Usually, Wil's certainty, his *adamancy* encouraged her, but not this time. And so, her purgatory become an even lonelier place.

Not long afterward, in the middle of one of a succession of sleepless nights, the acronym for the doctor's diagnosis, "GOD," burst into Maggie's consciousness. In that instant, she was reminded of who had given her this little boy and who trusted in her to care for him. In the glow of this realization, Robby's "disorder," a word she vowed never to use, wasn't a burden, a punishment, or even just a responsibility, but a gift, for which she felt honored and, strangely, worthy. She would not send him away to be made normal; she would keep him with her and teach him to be good at being unusual. After all, she used to teach ESL at the Community Center in Dorchester, where most of her adult students were never going to speak, read, or write English fluently, but with her help, they learned to do it all imperfectly well enough.

And so, for once, Maggie took issue with Wil.

"I don't want to send him away," she said—no, announced—the next night at dinner. "I want to take care of him at home. I'm . . ."

She sat impassively as Wil, quick and sharp with words as a major-league shortstop with a hard line drive, attempted to cut her off with a barrage of counterpoints. Again, she heard his adamancy, and then she replied with her own.

"I know what's best. I'm his *mother.*"

Wil's jaw dropped, as if he had just seen his unathletic wife beat out a throw to first base.

Maggie braced herself for a rebuttal, but all Wil did was shake his head and leave the room without another word. She could almost hear an umpire shout, "Safe!"

As she had expected, Wil did not back down, but neither did she. The impasse that ensued prompted the then-lucid Edna to dust off her collective-bargaining prowess, which, aided by a plethora of prayers, produced an alternative solution, the day program for special children at Saint Theresa's, right there in Chestnut Hill. With the stagey enthusiasm of a recruiter reciting a script, Edna assured Maggie and Wil that Robby would learn "skills of daily living and social interaction" in a "structured, but cognitively stimulating environment" for eight hours a day and still maintain his "essential family bond" evenings and weekends.

"The Ladies' Sodality and I have been storming heaven on this one, people, and . . ." She paused dramatically before declaring, "Saint T's is the answer we got."

Edna convinced Wil that a split decision was as good as he was going to get, but Maggie resisted it until Sweety weighed in, this despite the fact that her father had gone to his eternal reward not long after Mutti and Rosamund. In life, whenever he sensed that Maggie was feeling the pressure of Mum's Way, he tried to ease it with homespun aphorisms and homemade baked goods.

"Mum's Way's like broccoli, Mags; it can be hard to swallow, but you'll be glad ya did . . . someday. How about a cream puff?"

"You might get satisfaction if ya *don't* do it Mum's Way, Mags, but I say, what's satisfaction without a moment's peace? Here, have another brownie."

"Sure, ya give up somethin' goin' Mum's Way, Mags, but ya give up somethin' whenever ya donate to the needy. This cake turned out pretty good, huh?"

He had continued to counsel Maggie in the afterlife, through what she secretly called "Sweety Dreams." Although by now a less-than-devout Catholic and only third-generation Irish, Maggie had learned to recognize a sign from heaven when she saw one. And whenever she really, *really* needed it, she saw one. Sure enough, Maggie's first deep sleep since Robby's evaluation produced a beauty.

Maggie was kneeling between home plate and first base on a frozen infield afloat in rough, gray water, chipping away at the ice with a trowel and planting seeds. As quietly as a snowflake, a helicopter landed in the on-deck circle, and from it emerged a tall, burley man, his face stunningly black atop a white choir robe. He strode to the plate, where he surveyed the scene with Patton-like command.

"You're Diego Ortega," Maggie said to him, "the Red Sox batting star!"

He replied to her only with a smile, as brilliant as the snow, and then as if ready to battle the elements, he spat into one leather-gloved palm, slapped it against the other, and pulled a burlap sack out of the frosty air. Maggie watched as he lumbered past her and rounded the base paths, dipping his hand again and again into the sack and flinging its contents in every direction. When he had finished the circuit, he presented her with the empty sack before raising his arms and directing his eyes and both index fingers heavenwards.

Maggie looked up, expecting to see something celestial. But the dark, heavy clouds did not part, nor did a golden shaft of light emanate from them. When her gaze fell, though, she saw that the infield had sprouted a meadow brimming with tiny chrysanthemums, on which a pure white lamb was grazing.

"What's your secret?" she asked Ortega, but when she turned toward him, she found that he and the copter were gone.

When Maggie woke up, every detail of the dream was as sharp and clear as an instant replay on their new HD television. The meaning of it, though, was a different matter, as Sweety Dreams often were. A simple, straightforward man on earth, her father riddled his messages from the other side with symbolism reminiscent of countless, endless, nights in high school when Maggie, embattled by Vergil, Shakespeare, and Dickinson would cry out to her father, "Why don't they just say what they mean!"

To which he would reply, "Well, I don't know for sure, Mags, but I guess they wouldn't be poets if they did. Say, you look like you could use a cookie."

Two days after the dream, she was pretty sure that the lamb represented Robby and the icy baseball diamond her standoff with Wil and Edna, but the presence of Diego Ortega and the absence of Sweety, who had always given himself at least a cameo role in his productions, stymied her, until she picked up the sports section of the *Globe* off the bathroom floor. On the front page, surrounded by his smiling teammates, was a photo of Ortega, wearing a white apron and a chef's hat and holding a pan of muffins. The headline read: "Designated Baker."

In an instant, Maggie's brain cells were firing like an English major's. Her dream Ortega was Sweety! He made the tiny chrysanthemums grow on the ice! Tiny mums! Little Flower! Saint Theresa! Mum's Way!

By the end of the week, she and Wil had signed Robby up with Sister Esther, the principal of Saint Theresa's, and the following Monday, the school van came to pick him up.

♦ ♦ ♦

As Maggie dozed in the rocking chair, Edna watched her the way she used to more than three decades earlier.

"What a sweet face," she whispered. "She looks like somebody I used to know."

Quietly, she stood up and looked around for the baby quilt Sweety's mother had made, but all she found was a small scatter rug, which she gently placed on Maggie's lap.

With a start, she checked the wristwatch that she could no longer read.

"Oh, dear! I'm late. I'd better scoot, or they'll wonder where I am."

She scurried to the kitchen, where she searched the cabinets and drawers before pulling a small box from under the sink.

"Perfect!" she said. "I'm sure they'll *love* these."

On her way down the hall, she softly sang a tune her mother had taught her long ago.

When I grow too old to dream,
I'll have you to remember.
When I grow too old to dream,
Your love will live in my heart.

When she reached the coat rack in the entryway, she laid the box on the table and put on her gray tweed coat. Then, parcel in hand, she slipped out the front door.

3 - Telemachus and Athena

A few miles away, in the parking lot of the Shops at Chestnut Hill, Billy Nee sat in his car, watching well-heeled suburbanites dressed for yesterday's summerlike weather sprinting through a sudden early-spring snow squall: a yoga type wearing those stupid leggings that stop just below the knee and a blousy top with holes in the shoulders, a silver-haired couple decked out for a June wedding, and a middle-aged Masters Tournament wannabe in a green linen jacket and pale-yellow chinos. In contrast, Billy, who, as his mother had taught him, always listened to the WBZ weather report before leaving the house, was wearing a heavy-weight parka.

"Dumb shits," he muttered, and his smirky smile widened uncharitably.

Once the satisfaction of being smarter than rich people had subsided, Billy passed the time counting BMWs and Mercedes. After ten minutes, the Beemers were ahead seven to five. Not surprisingly, a car like his own was nowhere to be seen—a Ford Pinto that twenty-seven years and eight owners, Billy included, had not been kind to. With the edges of its headlight-eyes bandaged with duct-tape and its hood ajar like a mouth struggling to speak, the rust-spotted vehicle looked as if it were begging for a quiet corner in a scrap-metal yard or a vacant lot—any place where it wouldn't stick out so loudly.

By the time the tally reached twelve to eight, Billy caught the vibe of his car, and a surge of envy settled in the back of his throat. He tried clearing it a couple of times, as if he could dislodge the feeling like phlegm, even though he knew that this tactic never worked. He was trying to revert to the scorn he had enjoyed a few minutes earlier when a silver Jaguar zoomed into the space to his left, its stereo thumping.

"Asshole," he muttered.

This expletive succeeded only in making Billy feel like a hypocrite, because if he had the kind of dough this guy had, he would buy a Jaguar, too, to go with his Beemer and Mercedes.

He stole a glance at the driver and was surprised to see the guy staring at him. Then the Jag's front passenger window lowered. The guy couldn't have read his lips, and even if he had, what was he going to do—call him out for a duel? Diss the Pinto? The driver made a circular motion with his hand, signaling Billy to roll his window down. Billy was not a great one for doing as he was told, especially when rich assholes were doing the telling, and so the window stayed put. His pulse quickened when the guy got out of his car and hustled his sizable frame—6'4" if it was an inch—over to Billy's door. Billy cranked his window down as much as he could until the handle got stuck, and he was about to tell the guy to get the hell out of his face.

"Billy Nee!" his visitor exclaimed, bending over to see inside the car. "It *is* you! How the hell are you, man?"

He was wearing a parka, too, but there was a Woolrich Gortex label on the breast pocket. He looked like a young Matthew McConaughey, or maybe a catalogue model. These comparisons did not help Billy figure out how he knew this guy, which he obviously must. He hated situations like this, when somebody else knew what he didn't.

"I've changed, right?" the guy asked with a smile worthy of a toothpaste ad.

"Yeah," Billy managed to say. "And I guess I haven't."

"Oh, no. It's not that. I just never forget a face, and I'm pretty good with names, too."

"And I obviously suck at both, so . . . ?"

"Oh . . . yeah, sorry. Drew Winston." When no recognition registered on Billy's face, he added, "Shady Grove Academy? Ninth-grade English class?"

Billy conjured up an image of a chubby, deer-eyed squirt with braces, but the idea that that kid had turned into this Adonis was freakish. He didn't realize that his mouth was agape until Drew laughed.

"I guess it is a jaw dropper if you didn't see it happen."

"Yeah . . . well, so how's it goin'?"

"Cold right now," Drew replied, as he looked up at the snow swirling around him. "You want to go grab coffee or something?"

"I'm kind of waiting for somebody."

"Mind if I come in then?"

Billy did mind. The crap-filled interior of the Pinto was fine by him; in fact, he preferred it that way because it pretty much fit in with his life. It was a visual expression of it, really. Suddenly, though, he felt embarrassed by it, and embarrassment was right up there with envy and cluelessness on his emotional shit list. He was tempted to follow his father's ethic and blow this guy off, but it was his deceased mother's voice he heard in his head: "*There's never an excuse for rudeness, Billy.*" He went with a combo of parental influences.

"Nah, whatever," he replied, shrugging.

Once Drew had squeezed into the passenger seat, he looked around, then turned toward Billy and gave him the smile again. Billy expected an ironic comment, like "Nice car," but either

Drew was nonjudgmental about grime and clutter, or he was following his own mother's

politeness policy.

"So, how long has it been, man—nine, ten years?" Drew asked.

"Haven't counted," Billy replied.

"What have you been up to?"

"Oh, y'know, work."

If asked for details, Billy was prepared to say "sales," which wouldn't have been a lie. He'd been employed at Eddie Jack's Old Time Superette on Dorchester Avenue for going on five years. Sure, he mostly stocked shelves, sliced cold cuts, and filled in at the register, but he could also claim to be a marketing consultant. After all, he was the one who'd convinced Eddie to add "Old Time" to the store's name and to put some vintage black-and-white photographs in the windows so that the condo-yuppies in the neighborhood would think the place was retro-chic, and not what it really was—carelessly unrefurbished since 1962. He would have felt like a shit-phony trying to impress Drew, but that was what embarrassment did to you.

To avoid compromising himself, he asked, "You?"

"Oh, college, business school. Now I'm at Dodge Wyndham, the investment firm," Drew said in a flat tone. "But don't think I'm bragging. It's not as impressive as it might sound. My uncle's the 'Dodge,' so it wasn't too hard to get the job, you know?"

Billy didn't know. He could only imagine. And clear his throat.

"I don't see myself there for too long, though," Drew continued. "Funny, it's just the kind of work I trained for, but I'm already wondering if it's going to fulfill me. I mean, I'm good enough at it, but I have this nagging feeling that at some deeper level, it's just not right for me."

Billy thought that people who talked about self-fulfillment and deeper levels were annoying wimps who needed to grow up and shut up, but he was aware of his eavesdropping mother, so he kept his opinion to himself.

"Another part of the problem," Drew explained, "is that this job pays the bills pretty well, so who knows?"

Problem? Pretty well? Billy thought, glancing at the Jag.

Drew picked up an empty bag of cheese curls off the floor.

"I love these things," he said, and then with a quick, forced-sounding laugh, "I just wish I loved wealth management, too."

When Billy saw Drew settle back into the seat and heard his wistful sigh, he wished he hadn't said that he was waiting for someone. The truth was keeping him from telling a lie that would get him out of there: "*Jeez, look at the time! I've got to rush off now to catch a plane to Cancun.*"

"I feel like I'm caught in a . . . a . . . an existential dilemma," Drew said, still looking at the bag. "Do I take a chance and try to find a meaningful job, or do I just submit to the golden handcuffs?"

"Yeah, that's always a tough one," Billy replied, eyeing the Jag again.

Without looking up, Drew nodded and said, "It really is. It might be easier if I knew what *would* fulfill me, but I don't have a clue."

He suddenly turned and looked straight into Billy's eyes.

"What's my *goal*? My *vision*? My *passion*? I'm supposed to know by now, aren't I? I'm almost twenty-five! I sure hope it's not just money. How depressing would *that* be?" Drew moaned.

Billy had an instantaneous urge to pound this guy, who apparently didn't realize that addressing these questions, even rhetorically, to someone wearing a cheap jacket from Target in an old piece-of-shit car might not be cool. And although Billy didn't have much experience with emotional unburdening, he didn't see it as something you foist on a virtual stranger, except maybe a bartender when you're totally hammered, or in his father's case, when you beat the crap out of anyone who pisses you off.

His irritation subsided, though, as soon as he noticed something familiar in Drew's face, something Billy had seen in his own bathroom mirror a lot lately. For a while after it had first appeared, he didn't know what to think of it, except that he didn't like it. Then he read an article about people who were in the early stages of dementia—how they could find themselves someplace and have no idea where they were or why they were there or how they got there. It was a frighteningly apt description of how his mirror face made him feel. Ever since then, whenever Billy saw it, he immediately told himself that he was in the bathroom of his apartment on Maseley Street in Dorchester, washing up before he went to work at Eddie's and that if he didn't hurry up, his father would be banging on the door bellowing that he had to take a shit—all by way of proving that he was not losing his mind. But a question persisted: Why did it feel so much like it? He responded to it as he did to all types of emotional distress—by turning away and doing something else.

Now he reached into the back seat, riffled around a few seconds, and produced an unopened bag of cheese curls, which he handed to Drew.

"Here," he said.

"Thanks, man."

Drew opened the bag and held it out to Billy, who declined the offer.

"It's not that I have anything against money," Drew said, pausing to snarf the cheese curls.

Impressed, Billy turned his head away and smiled. He had pegged the guy as a nibbler.

"I mean, money's like the grand patriarch of my family. Everybody loves it—*reveres* it, really—and I didn't think I was any different. But I don't know, lately I think I might be."

He balled up the bag, looked around, and tossed it into the back seat. Billy nodded approvingly.

"I heard from this buddy of mine from college," Drew told him. "He's an orthopedic surgeon with Doctors Without Borders in Nigeria. Last week a woman showed up at the clinic and needed an emergency hysterectomy. I mean, she was going to die if she didn't get it right away. So, my buddy skyped his sister, who's an OB/GYN in New York, and she talked him through the surgery. They saved the woman's life!"

Billy guessed where this story was going but resisted the temptation to beat Drew to the punch.

"Meanwhile, do you know what *I* did last week? I worked with some slick, overpaid CEO on his stock portfolio. I help the rich get richer! I'm a freakin' cliché!"

He snuffled, and his eyes welled up. At the first sign of a tear, Billy was going to cut this whack-job off.

"You're probably thinking I'm some kind of whack-job for telling you all this," Drew said, "especially since we've been out of touch so long."

Billy was on the verge of blurting out, "Hell, yeah!" when Mum in his head erupted: "*BILLY!*"

Instead, he replied, "Just . . . curious."

"It's because you were the only person I could talk to back in ninth grade—about how miserable I was. Remember?"

Billy didn't remember, but if he had set a precedent for today's outpouring, he might never forgive himself.

"Everybody else at that school was scary smart, and I could barely keep up with the work.

I knew damn well the only reason I'd gotten in was that my dad and uncle were alums who'd basically bankrolled the new gym," Drew continucd.

Drew looked contemplatively out the window; Billy glanced impatiently at his watch.

"Remember that English presentation on *The Odyssey* Mr. Barber assigned us: 'Telemachus, Lost and Found?'" Drew asked. "He must have paired me with you because he knew I'd need help, which, of course, I did. When I told you I didn't know how Telemachus could be lost if he was at home with his mother, you said to think of the other meanings of the word. So I said, 'I'm lost at this school, and I'm really lost reading this book,' and you explained that that's exactly how Telemachus felt, what with the father he'd never met off fighting the Trojans for twenty years and all those creeps hitting on his mother and camping out in her house, and how it all made the kid feel confused and helpless and lonely, until the goddess gave him the balls to stand up for himself."

Billy's throat tightened as a recollection he had long since trashed came into focus.

"Long story short, not only did we ace the presentation, but I also finally felt that someone understood me. And after that, I just started unloading on you. I remember that you never tried to give me advice. You just sat there and let me talk, like you've been doing now, which was just what I needed. I really got to depend on you, and then after summer vacation when I found out you weren't coming back, I thought I'd be lost again. But you know what? I wasn't. I felt . . . better about myself, and my grades went up little by little. And somehow, even back then, I knew you had a lot to do with it. I mean, you were, like, as smart as anybody in the class, and this cool kid from the city, too. Maybe I figured that I couldn't be as worthless as I thought if you were my friend."

He reached over and gave Billy's arm a squeeze. Billy tried to summon his reliable shield of cynicism, but for once, he couldn't. What he felt instead was another wave of empathy, this one stronger and more seductive, and with it, the desire to return the gesture. He resisted it by bracing himself for the question he was sure was coming: *Why did you leave?*

Drew said only, "You helped me through a tough time, man, just like that goddess helped Telemachus. What was her name?"

"Athena," Billy replied quietly.

"Right, Athena. And when I saw you just now, it all came rushing back, and I guess I wanted it to happen again."

Billy wanted to say that Drew had helped him, too, that listening to his worries about not belonging made him feel less alone in his own. He wanted to tell him how much he hated being the poor kid in their class, the one who took a bus, a trolley, and a subway train to and from school while everyone else got picked up in cars that cost three times what his parents made in a year. He wanted to confess that the nicer people were to him, the more he felt like a charity case and the more he resented them. Above all, he wanted to finally admit that if it hadn't been for Drew, who voiced the kinds of feelings Billy stifled, he would have bailed long before he did. He heard his mother's voice encouraging him: "*Good, Billy, good! Go ahead—say it! SAY IT!*"

But he didn't.

"And who knows?" Drew said, breaking the silence. "Maybe it will."

"Yeah, well, I . . . hope so," Billy said, immediately struck by the inadequacy of his reply.

"Hey, I'll let you know. What's the best way to get in touch with you?"

Billy, not sure whether he wanted to reprise this meeting, said, "Um . . . it might be better if I called you. You got a card or something?"

Drew fished one out of his wallet. As he handed it to Billy, he said, "We could get together for beers or something. I bet there are some great bars in your neck of the woods."

An image of Drew on a stool at the Bantry Bay, surrounded by Billy's father and his fellow deadbeats made Billy smile.

"Yeah, that'd be fun."

"Well, I'd better haul," Drew said. "I've got to grab a couple of things before I pick up my Uncle Press and head to Maine. We're skiing up at Sunday River this weekend."

He held out his hand for a goodbye handshake, which Billy obliged him, relieved that it wasn't a hug.

"Later, man," Drew said.

"Yeah . . . later."

Drew got out of the car and hurried to the mall entrance, where he stopped to wave goodbye before disappearing inside. Billy wanted nothing more than to find the closest bar, the darker and dingier the better, but then he remembered why he was there. As if on cue, the van he was waiting for turned into the parking lot entrance. Billy saw it, lowered his head until it rested on the steering wheel, and groaned.

4 - Road Trippers

The driver of the van was Billy's best friend, Joe Doherty, whom Billy had known since first grade and envied since fifth. By that time, the boys were as close as brothers, united in suffering at the hands of men who had no business being fathers.

The bond began one afternoon outside Eddie Jack's Superette when the boys were in third grade. Joe was approaching the store as Leo Nee and Billy were leaving it. Leo thrust a bulging grocery bag at Billy, who was already carrying a smaller one, and then lit a cigarette. When Billy fumbled the load and dropped both bags, Leo shouted, "You goddamn fuckin' wimp!" and whacked him on the side of his head.

The next day in the schoolyard at recess, Joe whispered to Billy, "What your father called you yesterday? Mine calls me that all the time. He hits me, too."

From then on, the boys listened to each other's latest accounts of mistreatment, cursed the offenders, and planned schemes of revenge they knew they would never carry out for fear of reprisal, but that made them at least feel bold. When

Leo called Billy a "slow shit" for not bringing him and his poker buddies their beers fast enough, the boys imagined adding piss or castor oil, or both, to it the next time. Soon afterward, when Jake Doherty deliberately tripped Joe on the sidewalk and then called him a "fuckin' little klutz," they envisioned greasing the front steps with motor oil just before he staggered home from the Bantry Bay.

Then Jake had the surprising decency to croak from a heart attack incurred during a bar fight before he could complete the job of grinding down his son's self-esteem, a mission that the perversely resilient Leo, who had ample opportunities to croak in bar fights, continued to pursue unabated.

All the while, Billy's mother, Betty, a devout Catholic, had long since realized that her marriage vow "to have and to hold, for better and for worse, till death do us part . . ." had stuck her with a mean-spirited loser. In a sincere but naïve attempt to compensate for the nastiness he dumped on their son, she devoted her life to Billy in every way she could think of. She encouraged him to try the things she knew he wanted to try but was afraid to, like auditioning for a part in the Saint Aloysius CYO's production of *Grease*. She worked extra shifts in the kitchen at the Kearney Hospital so that she could buy him a cell phone like all the other kids at Shady Grove had. Most of all, she drew out from him the hurt Leo had inflicted and talked with Billy about it and assured him that he was a good boy, "the best boy ever." When he wasn't ready to talk, she brought him snack packs of cheese curls and hugged him. What she didn't do—what she believed the sacrament of marriage precluded—was the thing that would have helped Billy the most: leaving the bastard and taking Billy with her.

And then one stifling August night when Billy was fifteen, just as Betty was completing her shift at the hospital, her loving heart seized up, the victim of hereditary arrhythmia syndrome. By the time Billy and Leo arrived, she was gone, leaving her son alone with the stinker she had been trying to shield him from.

Joe did what he could to fill the gap, inviting Billy over for dinners and sleepovers several times a week. Billy always accepted, even though seeing Joe with his devoted mother made the loss of his own more acute.

There were times, though, when Billy felt that Mrs. Doherty overdid her encouragement, especially when Joe, who was taking an art class at the community center, revealed a new painting. "It's perfect, Joey, *per*fect!" was her unfailing response, no matter how imperfect the work was. When Billy was present, he felt obliged to echo her praise, although he toned it down to "Wow, man!" or "That's really something." It wasn't that he knew much about art, but he had seen some really cool stuff that kids at Shady Grove had done, and in comparison, Joe was missing something. The Leo in Billy thought, "*Yeah, talent,*" to which his Mum side countered, "*No, no . . . but maybe a little shading and . . . what do they call it? Proportion?*"

Whatever the source of the problem was, Joe's paintings were, in his friend's eye, just too simple, only a step above the pictures Billy used to bring home from Saint A's and his mum hung up on the fridge.

Joe became further deluded in senior year when his young, lustful art teacher, Ms. "Call me Miranda" Rheinbeck, gushed over his "passionate eye" and "sinewy strokes"—so deluded that he applied to art schools. Predictably, to Billy anyway, none accepted him.

Undeterred, Joe enrolled in an evening art program at a community college. With unflagging optimism, he stayed the course, got his certificate, and followed his muse to a vacant classroom at Saint Anthony's Elementary School. There, he set up a studio and threw himself into his work with gleefulness that struck Billy as unbecoming a struggling artist. The irony that at Saint Anthony's Joe was surrounded by other producers of fridge-art in a building dedicated to the Patron Saint of Lost Causes gave his best friend perverse satisfaction.

For almost three years, Joe had carted samples of his love's labor to every art venue within a 100-mile radius and despite anemic sales numbers, had maintained robust optimism. Not so, Mrs. Doherty. Joe's meager contribution to household expenses finally stretched the cord of her generosity to the snapping point, resulting in a thinly veiled ultimatum.

"Ya art stuff's . . . beautiful, Joey. Real beautiful. But it don't help with the bills. This job I got ya at Mrs. Dobrowski's brother-in-law's van company, now that *will* help with the bills."

Six weeks of quasi-compliance later, during which Joe shuttled special needs children to Saint Theresa's School and home again, Joe got another talking-to, this one decidedly unveiled, from Mrs. Dobrowski's brother-in-law, Vin of "Vin's Vans" at Fields Corner in Dorchester.

"I don't give a shit about ya pretty little pitchiz, kid. I get one more call from Sister What's Her Face, tellin' me you missed a run, I fire your ass."

Thus warned, Joe found himself in a bind that week when Miranda, who had evaded prosecution for child seduction, found an art fair at a ski resort in Maine, where Chestnut

Hill types might cap off a day on the slopes by shopping for rudimentary watercolors. As he usually did when he faced a dilemma, Joe called Billy, who quickly devised the stratagem of Joe's picking the kids up at school (to prevent the principal, Sister Esther, from ratting him out to Vin) and then handing them off to Billy in the mall parking lot. After the last drop-off, Billy would get the van back to Vin's after the office closed at five thirty, so Vin wouldn't know that Joe had engaged an unauthorized substitute.

"But that means you'll have to take the T all the way back to Chestnut Hill to get the Pinto," Joe pointed out.

"Anything for a friend, Joe boy," Billy replied, "and for the arts, of course."

♦ ♦ ♦

Joe parked two rows away, and Billy walked over to meet him. As soon as he reached the van, a silver Jaguar zipped into a nearby space, making Billy think that Drew was stalking him. When Miranda alighted from the car with a signature swoosh of her flowing brown hair, he was almost relieved.

"Hi, Billy," she purred. Miranda always reminded Billy of a cat. Billy hated cats.

"Hey," he muttered, avoiding eye contact. He had just caught sight of her ass, inviting attention in jeans so tight they looked as if they'd been painted on, but he resisted the temptation to take another look.

The ensuing silence was broken when Joe emerged from the van. Billy noticed with a start what an uncanny resemblance his friend bore to Drew Winston—same imposing height, same sturdy build, same movie-star cheekbones.

Surprisingly, Joe's strapping good looks had never aroused envy for Billy to cough up, although he was just shy of five-nine with the slight frame of a distance runner. Credit for this bit of self-acceptance went to his mother.

"You're cute and smart, Billy," she told him time and again. "Girls like cute and smart."

Her assessment proved correct. Girls in the neighborhood and at Shady Grove flirted aggressively with him, but Billy's chronic shyness, a by-product of his father's disparagement, made sure they got little satisfaction. When Patty Linehan, on whom Billy had an intense crush, invited him to the Sadie Hawkins dance, he was simultaneously filled with delight and panic. Panic won out.

"Um," he told her, "I think I'm busy."

Miranda, however, unencumbered by social shyness, immediately flung herself into Joe's arms and initiated a way-too-long kiss, during which Billy surveyed the cloudy sky.

"Billy," Joe finally said. "Thanks for this, bro."

"Sure," Billy replied, impatient for the two huggers to unpeel themselves from each other. Public displays of affection always bugged him, but he suspected that this was just another envy thing.

He cleared his throat and asked, "So . . . you got the list?"

Joe pulled a sheet of paper from his jacket pocket and handed it to Billy.

"As promised," he said proudly.

When Billy was formulating the plan, he saw that he couldn't rely on a bunch of mentally impaired kids to know their addresses. He told Joe to get him a list of them, or else the plan was toast. As it turned out, the secretary at Saint Theresa's gave Joe an updated one every day because parents often picked their kids up for various appointments. The printout, cut and pasted from the school directory, had the names, photos, addresses, and phone numbers of the kids Joe would be driving home on any given day.

Longing even more now to get to a bar, Billy was disappointed that Joe had come through, but he managed to say, "Yeah, well . . . good then."

"It *is* good, Bill. The whole thing's good. I'm channeling some real positive energy today. *Real* positive. I just know that somebody up there is gonna smile upon my work."

At first, Billy thought this was a reference to divine intervention, which he considered the only thing that could make Joe's crazy dreams come true, but he quickly realized that his friend was referring to skiers in Maine. Simultaneously, he had a surge of nostalgia for pre-Miranda Joe, who never spoke of "channeling positive energy," but of "getting pumped" and "kicking ass," almost always in the context of football and baseball.

"They'll be smiling all right," Billy replied with ironic intent that morphed into sympathy for his friend, who he was sure, was on the verge of another failure.

Eager to get the whole thing over with, he shifted gears.

"So, anyway, should you, like, introduce me to the kids?"

"Oh, right," said Joe.

He slid the door of the van open.

"Hey, road-trippers, listen up," Joe announced. "This is my buddy, Billy. You're goin' the rest of the way with him today."

Billy had heard Joe's accounts of the kids' behaviors but until that moment thought they were exaggerated.

When he stuck his head inside to see his passengers, he was greeted with chanting: "Bunny Belly. Bunny Belly. Bunny Belly."

He was greeted with song: "BILLY, don't be a HERO, don't be a FOOL with your life . . ."

He was greeted with demands: "Want peanuts. Get peanuts."

He was greeted with questions—lots of questions:

"You know the zip code for East Providence, Rhode Island 02914?"

"Where *is* Dick Cheney?"

"When will it be eighty-one degrees?"

All this emanated from the vocal members of the group. A nonverbal contingent grunted, giggled, or gasped. A silent minority stared blankly, some drooling, some swaying their heads.

"So, what do you think?" Joe asked him.

"I think you're pickin' up the tab at the Connemara next week."

"You got it."

Miranda interrupted their conversation. Billy discovered that she could whine as well as purr.

"Baby, I'm getting chilly," she said.

Joe hurried over to her and enveloped her in another hug.

"I'm sorry, Cuddles. I guess we ought to get our road trip going, too."

They gazed into each other's eyes. Billy rolled his. Pre-Miranda Joe never called anybody

"Cuddles."

Joe grabbed a duffel from the van and tossed it into the trunk of the Jag.

Billy felt richly deserving of a parting dig despite the disapproving tone of Mum in his head: "*Bil-ly, don't!*"

"Nice car, Miranda. The teachers' union must have scored a big raise this year, huh?"

She shot him a feline grin.

"It was more than adequate."

"Oh, she didn't buy it," Joe said. "Her father gave it to her when she turned thir . . ."

"Let's *go*, baby." Miranda snarled as Billy basked in snarky satisfaction.

By the time he got behind the wheel of the van, though, he was clearing his throat. Resilient, hopeful Joe, with his hot girlfriend, was heading off in a cool sports car in pursuit of a lofty dream, while Billy was stuck schlepping the odd squad for the next two hours through Friday afternoon traffic, after which he would have to schlep himself for another hour to retrieve his crappy car if it hadn't been towed.

"*Come on, Billy,*" Mum in his head urged him. "*Try channeling some positive energy. I'll send you some!*"

He closed his eyes and took a deep breath, then another and another, waiting for an upbeat thought to pop into his head like a text message notification. After the fourth breath, all he came up with was: *Maybe this won't be so bad.*

"*But that's not what I . . .*" Mum in his head tried to say before she was interrupted by a quartet of road trippers.

"Want peanuts! Want peanuts!"

"One penis. One penis. One penis . . ."

"Do you know the zip code for Terre Haute, Indiana 47801?"

"INDIANA wants me, LORD, I can't go back there. INDIANA wants me, LORD, I can't go back there . . ."

"Sorry, Mum," Billy said. "It's a lost cause."

5 - Irish Eyes

"Dodgeball!"

Wil Dodge usually loved hearing his editor, Barney Killian, call out the nickname he had coined for him years ago, even though its original intent was not kind. When Wil joined the *Globe* sports staff, Killian made it clear that he considered him a lightweight, hired only because Wil's uncle had gone to Harvard ("Hahvid," as Killian pronounced it) with the publisher. Since then, Wil's talent and doggedness had earned Killian's respect. It was grudging at first, but now it felt to Wil almost affectionate.

Killian's tone now, though, was decidedly unaffectionate, and Wil knew why.

"Be right in, boss," he called out and then sat staring at the coffee mug in his hand, as if it might transmit the luck of the Irish, or at least some plausible blarney, which was what he needed for the impending inquisition.

The kelly-green mug, one of his favorite possessions, was inscribed in white lettering with the words: *Honorary Harp*. It was a gift from the family of his college roommate, Tommy Joyce, with whom he had spent a blissful, cathartic summer almost seventeen years earlier, a summer that accomplished Wil's goal of escaping, at least temporarily, from the affluent lifestyle he had grown up with.

Wil had been quite comfortable with that lifestyle until a few months earlier, when he brought Tommy home to Marblehead for Prescott Dodge's fiftieth birthday and caught his friend grinning at odd times, as if someone were whispering snide comments into his ear. It happened over cocktails on the oceanfront patio, at the black-tie dinner at the club, and on the yacht. On their way back to Amherst, Wil, with uncharacteristic tentativeness, asked Tommy if he'd had a good time.

"Good? Dodgey, it was awesome!" Tommy replied and then upped the compliment to its highest degree. "Wicked awesome!"

Convinced that he had misread the grins, Wil relaxed, until Tommy continued.

"I mean, I always figured you were from money, big guy—not that you're stuck up or anything, but I didn't know you were . . . magazine people!" Tommy said.

He said it uncritically, admiringly, even, and yet the phrase released in Wil a hot flash of humiliation because when he was thirteen years old, his family had, in fact, been featured in a magazine, the Christmas issue of *Fine Family Living*. The stylist, Margot, a statuesque blonde who always smiled and wore pink had teamed up with Jazmine, who was petite, fit, and grim-faced, like a goth-ish marathoner, to produce a four-page spread that showcased Ginger Dodge's crowning achievement: a picture-perfect home and a picture-perfect family.

Young Wil had long since resigned himself to the tyranny of household rules his mother had devised, the number of which grew each time he or his siblings, in the natural course of being children, sullied the work of art that was their—more accurately, her—home.

"New rule!" she would exclaim, as she grabbed a permanent-ink marker and scurried to add the newest prohibition to the list she kept posted on a whiteboard near the door of the mud room, the only entrance her children were allowed to use. All items were stifling, comprehensive, and punctuated to show that she meant business:

No outdoor behavior! This meant anything really fun.

No outdoor voices! This was the gateway to outdoor behavior.

No clutter! This proved to be open to interpretation as to what constituted clutter and where those items became clutter, and so the rule required frequent addenda and a second whiteboard:

This includes toys, stuffed animals, and games!

This includes crayons, pencils, pens, books, papers, and backpacks!

This includes jackets, hats, and all other clothes!

On the floor = Clutter!

On windowsills, doorknobs, stairways, and railings = Clutter!

On chairs, ottomans, and couches = Clutter!

Enduring the two-day photo shoot turned out to be only slightly more annoying than normal daily life for Wil. But seeing the results in glossy, high-definition color was a real oh-shit moment. And facing the ridicule of his buddies when they saw the magazine—and they *all* saw it because Mrs. Dodge had made sure that every mother in the PTA knew the publication date—was like stumbling upon a hive of wasps.

It would have been hard for Wil to say what photo brought him the most ridicule:

Wearing an apron embroidered with the word *JOY!* as he placed a gumdrop onto a gingerbread replica of the Dodges' house. "*Hey, Dodge! Your iddy biddy cookie house is so-pwitty!*"

In red uncut cords, a green vest, and a scotch-plaid bow tie standing under the mistletoe *with his sister.* "*Eeeeeew! Eeeeeeeeeew!*"

Hanging Christmas stockings by the fireplace with her and his little brothers. "*And what did Santa leave* you, *little boy?*"

And, as if to seal Wil's fate as a victim of early adolescent torture, the text described the children as "precious."

Wil had long suppressed this painful memory, but Tommy's remark released it. He did not want this cool, scrappy scholarship student from South Boston, the son of Lovey and Peg, a butcher and a hairdresser, to think he was precious. So, he wrangled an invitation to spend the summer with the Joyces in their three-decker on East Fourth Street, and for three months, he reveled in the life of his social antithesis, supermarket-circular people. He ate tuna noodle casseroles topped with potato chips and served with a side of canned green beans mixed with imitation bacon bits. He went to Sunday Mass at the Heavenly Gates Church and Wednesday night bingo in the parish hall. He sat in the *bleachers* at Fenway Park. He attended "times" at the VFW Post for neighbors retiring from the gas company or running for state representative. He even learned to operate a meat slicer, to lay linoleum, and to do his own laundry.

The highlight of Wil's summer, though, was grocery shopping with Peg, a round, rosy-faced sports lover who smiled at him with her bright, compassionate eyes and called him "Wil-hon." (The fact that she added the suffix to almost everyone's name didn't detract from Wil's delight whenever he heard it.) On the way from market to market—they hit at least four to capitalize on weekly specials—they chatted amiably about local teams: the Red Sox's chances of reversing the curse, the relative merits of Bill Belichick and Red Auerbach, and the Bruins' glory years of Orr and Esposito. As the weeks passed, though, Wil found himself going deeper, confiding in Peg, everything from the magazine fiasco to his dream of being a sportswriter and the impending collision it would almost certainly cause with his father's dream that he join the family's wealth management firm. Her attentiveness whenever he spoke was total, sympathetic, and encouraging. She never gave him judgments or advice, only nods and hugs, and he loved her for it all, like a son should love a mother.

Since then, Wil had returned to the affluence he once spurned, but the memories of that simple, lovely time lingered, and with it, a fondness for all things Irish Catholic. For this reason, he craved the approval of his florid, keg-bellied editor, the son of immigrants from County Roscommon, who worked his way through UMass Boston by driving a cab. Wil's favorite expression of Killian's support is "I guess I'm glad we hired your skinny, preppy ass after all." Gripping the mug now, Wil stood up and walked toward Killian's door, certain that he was not going to hear that sentence today.

♦ ♦ ♦

"Make me happy," Killian said, popping the last bite of a doughnut into his mouth. Wil saw two more atop a bakery bag on the desk. They looked like the filled kind.

"Well, if you mean, have I heard from him . . ."

"I mean 'have you heard from him,' and here's a hint: 'Yes' would make me happy."

"Not exactly."

"Then I'm exactly not happy." As if to compensate for his disappointment, Killian started in on another doughnut. Wil saw a yellow substance oozing out of it. *Lemon cream*, he thought.

"But I'm still sure . . ."

"Screw *sure,* Dodgeball. *Sure* doesn't get us the story. *Sure* doesn't beat the bastards at the *Herald. Sure* doesn't get you the book contract we both know you're aiming for." He thrust the doughnut forward, not to offer a bite, as Wil momentarily thought, but to emphasize his final point. "*Sure* doesn't do anything but shit the bed."

Wil was accustomed to Killian's rants; sometimes he even enjoyed the theatrics of them: the rising facial color, the tight jaw, the bellowing, and most of all, the glare. He had heard it likened to a double-barreled rifle aimed squarely at a hapless transgressor's eyes, but to Wil, it was always just part of the show. His nonchalance was due to the fact that he was almost always sure of himself, or if he weren't, he could at least convince people, himself included, that he was. As a result, disparagement and intimidation, however they were conveyed, just slid off him like raindrops on Gortex. But today he was getting soaked because he didn't have a clue, and he couldn't even fake it. It was a crappy feeling before Killian called him in, and it was even crappier facing him.

Wil found himself eyeing the remaining doughnut. It looked plump, sweet, and comforting, just like the kind that Peg Joyce used to bring home from Domenic's Bakery on K Street, and now that he thought of it, just like Peg Joyce herself. He had an urge to ask for it but wisely refrained, for Killian had apparently noticed Wil's covetous look and moved the bag closer to himself.

"You said you had a *rapport* with the guy, Dodgeball, that you were his *confidante.* Now, maybe I didn't go to Amherst, but I do know what those words mean. They mean he calls and tells you where the hell he is and why the hell he's there and not where he's supposed to be and when the hell he's coming back!"

Wil must have looked at the doughnut again because Killian grabbed it and took a hefty bite, even though half of the second one was still in his other hand.

"And if he doesn't call goddamn soon, and by that I mean *today*, then screw *rapport*, and screw *confidante* and go find him!"

"He'll call, Barney," Wil replied in what he hoped was a calming tone, but when he saw the glare deepen, he could almost hear the click of a shotgun, so he quickly added, "or I'll find him. Definitely. Definitely. I'll find him."

"Make it happen. Make me happy."

Wil considered saluting, just to lighten things up, but realized that the way his luck was running, the gesture would probably backfire. He just turned toward the door, but before he reached it, he heard Killian's final mandate and grinned.

"And get your own goddamn doughnuts."

6 - Sure

Wil sat at his computer, staring at a photo of a lanky young man in a Red Sox uniform—Eamon Lally, the "him" he had just been charged with finding. The picture showed Eamon on the mound, the Green Monster in the background, winding up to deliver his signature pitch, which the Fenway Faithful called The Lallypalooza. It was a bizarre journey of ball through air, which a class of physics students at MIT were assigned to explain and opposing batters struggled to hit—explosive, then languid; enticing, then elusive. In his first season with the Sox, the pitch got Lally an ERA of 2.90, a twenty-four to five record, and the AL Rookie of the Year award. Skeptics predicted that he couldn't possibly maintain those stats, but for the next two years, he did, earning the Cy Young as a result.

Wil was not one of the doubters and had early on declared Eamon a "godsend," an accolade he had never bestowed, even on slugger Diego Ortega, the heart and soul of the team. Wil had always considered the word trite, hyperbolic, and way too spiritual for a serious sportswriter, but Eamon had dispelled his objections, perhaps because it occurred to Wil that *Godsend* would be a great title for a book. Once he envisioned his name and the young hurler's photograph on its front cover, he became a believer in divine intercession.

First, though, he had to get the excruciatingly shy kid to open up to him, a feat that had stymied every sportswriter in town. Eamon answered most questions with "Yes," "No," or "Good," although occasionally he launched into two words: "Hope so," "Hope not," or "We'll see." Some writers had already given up on getting anything out of him. "It's like tryin' to get my wife to *stop* talking—goddamn impossible," one of them had grumbled. Wil persisted, though, because another bestseller hung in the balance.

With a click of the mouse, Wil now brought another image onto the screen, one of Eamon and himself in the Red Sox clubhouse. Wil was smiling broadly at the camera; Eamon was looking off to the side, too shy or modest for a full-on gaze. Even in semi-profile, it was a lean, boyish face, the kind that aroused in women both romantic and maternal instincts.

Wil recalled an evening about a year before the picture was taken, when the press corps was trooping out after yet another frustrating attempt at an interview. It was then that Wil spotted a book in Eamon's locker. Suddenly, he saw the clouds part and the dreamed-of cover of *Godsend* emerge, framed in gold. He tracked down a copy at a Catholic bookstore on Hawley Street, and on the next road trip held it open in front of his face when he saw Eamon coming up the aisle of the team plane. Wil glanced up long enough to see the rookie do a double-take, and sure enough, Eamon, apparently moved to find a sportswriter engrossed in *Inspiring Lives of Martyrs and Saints*, tentatively approached Wil at the airport.

"So . . . um . . . who's your favorite?" he asked without lead-in. "Saint, I mean."

Unfazed that his strategy had not involved actually reading the book, Wil replied, "Hmm. It's hard to choose. They're all so . . . saintly. Who's yours?"

"I'd have to go with Saint Sebastian, him bein' the patron of athletes, plus he survived all those arrows."

"Yeah, ya gotta like the guy's stamina."

"A'course they finally got him with their bloody rods and dumped him in the sewer, but I guess that was kind of a blessing because he wouldn't have been a martyr without dying a gruesome death."

"A blessing," Wil repeated, already itching to steer this weird conversation toward baseball, but smart enough to wait.

For a few weeks, he feigned interest as Eamon marveled over the "blessings" of Saint Blaise and Saint Perpetua and Saint Benignus—beheading, clubbing, and stabbing, respectively. And then one afternoon, after reflecting on Saint Victor—crushed by a millstone—Eamon said plaintively, "I wonder what it feels like . . ."

Wil stifled a groan.

"To be so sure of something. I mean, so sure, you'd be happy to sacrifice everything for it."

Sureness was something Wil could speak to. Sacrifice, though, he considered a quaint, counterintuitive notion, except in the case of a bunt. His reasoning ran along a simple, competitive line: you don't win if you lose. And yet, the wistfulness in Eamon's voice and the tenderness in his eyes aroused in Wil a wave of compassion and, inexplicably, a twinge of envy. His experience with these feelings was not extensive, but always unsettling because they made him feel vulnerable, and he hated feeling vulnerable almost as much as he hated losing. Caring too much about someone else's problems somehow released his own, especially the ones he didn't want to admit to. More troubling still, wishing he were more like someone else was like declaring his inferiority, or worse, defeat. He had become practiced in whisking away both feelings as if they were pesky mosquitoes.

When his guard was down, though, he sometimes got bitten. His mother-in-law could do it to him. He'd see her sitting in her rocking chair, smiling at him, probably wondering who he was, and immediately he felt himself drawn into her decline so entirely that it seemed as if it were happening to him.

What also got to him was his wife's devotion to Edna, and to Robby, too, selfless and loving.

"A saint," according to Barney Killian.

"When that wife of yours dies," he once told Wil, "she goes straight to the Hall. First ballot.

Unanimous vote."

Wil admired her, too—and yes, he wished he could be more like her—but was shamefully aware that for him, the responsibility she accepted so cheerfully was a burden he could barely endure even from the sidelines.

Whenever he succumbed to these thoughts, all the crap he liked to think he had under control blindsided him: that Edna, once as delightfully quick witted and sharp tongued as Killian, was as good as dead, that the son his genes had co-produced—worse, the son who looked just like him—was abnormal, *deficient*, and always would be. He wasn't going to play baseball or any other sport. He wasn't going to Amherst. He wasn't going to accomplish anything that Wil would feel proud of. As if that didn't make him feel bad enough, Maggie's goodness made him feel like a shit on top of a loser.

Listening to Eamon now, Wil succumbed to the urge to clamp the lid on Eamon's provocative musings. In a tone that sounded harsh, even to himself, he asked, "How the hell did you get into all of this?"

If Eamon picked up the offensive tone, he didn't show it. He only nodded, almost imperceptibly, as if responding to the flashing fingers of his catcher.

"It started around tenth grade, I guess, at Bishop Brandt High back in Wisconsin. That's when I got the book. It was a prize for 'Most Earnest Student.' I didn't even know what that meant, but I never got awards for anything except baseball, so I was kind of pumped. Sister Regina Joseph—she's the one who gave it to me—said it should help me find the 'God within.' Well, I knew what that meant because she was always going on about it—something about how God puts some of himself in everybody, but in different ways, and how everybody's got to find their particular God and y'know, do what he says. Looking for it didn't make sense for me, though, because even by that time, most everybody knew my God was a pitcher. I never thought about it much because I figured they must be right, so I put the book on a shelf with my trophies. Once in a while, I'd get the urge to read some of it, but it's only lately I've been really getting into it a lot and I don't know . . . thinking."

From the recesses of his memory, Wil heard Peg Joyce on the day he left South Boston: "*If the God within you is a sportswriter, Wil Dodge, you will have no choice but to be one.*"

With this recollection, compassion and envy vaporized, replaced by a fear that sucked Wil's rational mind into a lopsided debate with its counterpart:

Eamon never chose *to be a pitcher. He was just swept into it, and now he's having nun-induced doubts and wondering whether his God could be a social worker or some other kind of do-gooder!*

Unlikely, since . . .

Unlikely? So is getting off on martyrs!

He's just . . .

And if he finds the something else, he'll have no choice but to do it. Peg said so!

But she . . .

Shut the hell up and let me think!

Calm analysis thus stifled, Wil vowed not to take a chance; the Red Sox, their fans, and his readers needed him to use his influence to steer this wavering man-child away from moody introspection and to focus on the things that would help him succeed: balls and strikes, pitch counts and run support, wins and losses.

Being the compliant sort, Eamon followed Wil's lead, and for the remainder of that season and throughout the next, he talked the talk Wil asked for. Whenever Eamon got martyry, Wil listened attentively, just the way Peg used to listen to him, with eye contact and nods, but all the while waiting to pounce on a segue to baseball.

"Imagine a girl as young as Joan of Arc, younger than me even, getting burned at the stake rather than denying her faith."

"Unbelievable. And talk about getting burned—what's with the bullpen this year?"

In the middle of the next season, though, Eamon clammed up and worse, went into an extended slump that contributed to the Sox missing a playoff spot and spurred some fans to rename the Lallypalooza the "Lallypaloser." Wil tried to backdoor it again by asking the kid about martyrs, but even Saint Josaphat—axed by a mob—produced only a lackluster response. When Wil shifted to baseball, all Eamon said was, "Dunno. I guess maybe I'm just losing it."

During the off-season, Wil's anxiety roiled his nights like a string of nor'easters, generated by those last words: *Losing what? It can't be ability. Ability just doesn't disappear at age twenty-four! It's got to be focus or desire! Then what the hell is he focused on? What does he want? It's that goddamn God within, I tell you!*

In an attempt at damage control, Wil tried to stay in touch with Lally, who was ensconced with his parents at their home in Milwaukee. The first time Wil called on the phone, he was encouraged by Mrs. Lally's sweet brogue—older Irish women always loved him—but this one proved to be immune to his charms, a guard dog with total control of communication lines to her son.

"I thank you kindly for checkin' in on my boy, Mr. Dodge. And isn't that sweet of ya, remembering him in your prayers. But I tell ya, he's takin' a break from all that baseball stuff. I *strongly* suggest you do the same."

Spring training finally came, and Eamon showed signs of a return to his old form, prompting Wil to write a column entitled "Lallypalazarus" that he hoped would convince the fans and himself that the nightmare was over. Just after training camp broke, though, another nightmare ensued when Eamon disappeared.

As soon as Wil found out, he tried his luck with Mrs. Lally again, but despite his solicitousness, she was no more forthcoming and even more pointed than she had been a few months earlier.

"Sure, if it isn't dear of ya to be worried sick about my Eamon, Mr. Dodge. And makin' a novena for him, God love ya. But rest assured, he's in good hands in a good place. He's just got some decidin' to do. So, you just leave him be."

After Wil had reported this in his column, he got a call from Eamon's agent, the combustible Richie Buck, who was by then fully engulfed.

"IN *WHOSE* FUCKIN' HANDS? FUCKIN' *WHERE*? DECIDIN' FUCKIN' *WHAT*?" Richie screamed. And after a breath that sounded more like a gasp, "WHAT KIND OF FUCKIN' CLUELESS REPORTER *ARE* YOU?"

As Wil, still clueless, now stared at his computer screen, the phone rang. When he answered it, he heard Richie again, sounding preternaturally contained.

"Beat ya to him, Dodgeball."

"You *found* him?"

"Don't sound so surprised. I got people. They got ways. Which is a lot more than I can say about you."

"Well, where is he?" Wil, now on his feet, let the dig slide.

"In good hands. In a good place. Where else?" Wil could almost see Richie smirking.

"Cut the crap. Where the hell *is* he?"

"Saint Francis, my son."

"My God . . . he's in the *hospital*?"

"I wish," Richie replied with a yawn. "No, Dodgeball. Saint Francis *Seminary*."

Wil fell back into his chair. "WHAT!"

"Seems what he's deciding on is a career change. But he's willing to talk to you first. Says you understand him."

"Oh, Jesus," Wil moaned.

"Better not take the Lord's name in vain when you talk to Eamon. And you *will* talk to him, Dodgeball, in half an hour," Richie told him in a Barney Killian tone.

"Right. I'm on my way."

As he rushed out the door, cursing Sister Regina Joseph, another woman in black invaded his consciousness, Sister Esther of Saint Theresa's, with a reminder that he was supposed to pick Robby up at school and take him to the gym in forty-five minutes. She insisted that this weekly outing was vital for Robby—some edubabble about a father-son bond stimulating emotional cognition—but all Robby ever did was bounce a ball by himself for an hour, stimulating nothing more than Wil's shit-on-top-of-a-loser mindset. Skipping the trip once—okay, once again—wouldn't hurt the kid. It never did, right? Without further consideration, he pulled out his phone and called the school secretary, Mrs. Caggianelli, to get Robby's name back on the daily van list. He left voicemails for Maggie on both the house line and her cell and with his duties dispatched, redirected his mind to the current crisis.

In the elevator, though, a question disturbed his focus—why hadn't Maggie picked up either phone? She'd never take Edna out when her soaps were on. Even if she did, she'd have her cell with her. Maybe something was wrong . . . but Maggie handling a problem without turning to him for advice?

"Yeah, right," he muttered, rolling his eyes.

If anything was wrong, she'd call him. For sure.

7 - Mum's Away

Maggie's eyelids fluttered. Through halfway opened eyes, she saw an expanse of white and felt a chill. Where was she? Why was she so cold? The first question was answered when she recognized her snow-coated front yard through the living room windows, framed by the rosebud-pattern drapes her mother-in-law had chosen. But wait . . . she was inside, so it should be warm. Didn't they have replacement windows installed just last fall? Then why this cold draft, not to mention this scatter rug on her lap?

When she turned to her left and saw her mother's empty chair, reality opened her eyes wide and snapped her out of her post-nap disorientation.

"Mum?" she called, and when she got no reply, she repeated more loudly, "MUM?"

She stood up, letting the rug fall and hurried through the dining room to the kitchen, where she had sometimes found Edna trying to reprise her old role as supply manager and executive chef, cheerfully unaware of the absurdity of her endeavors. Once, she was whistling "Get Happy" from her favorite musical, *Summer Stock*, as she transferred the contents of the freezer to the oven. Another day, she was smiling like a model in an advertising shoot for cake mix as she stirred a bowl of water with a wooden spoon. On other occasions, though, Maggie caught her looking adrift in confusion. Most recently, Edna was standing at the counter and staring at the toaster, a piece of bread in her hand. Her eyebrows were furrowed, as if she were impatient for the appliance to tell her how it worked. When she looked up at Maggie, her expression changed, replaced by the I-know-the-score look of the old union rep, of the take-charge wife and mother. In that moment, though, it was etched with fear that told Maggie that her mother was aware of what she was losing.

"What happens now?" Edna practically whispered.

Maggie rushed forward and embraced her.

"I take care of you, Mum," she said. "That's what happens. I take care of you."

And she made good on the promise. She went with Edna to Mass every morning after Robby had left for school. She let her do chores, like putting away the silverware, even though it ended up jumbled. She sang show tunes with her and looked at pictures in cooking magazines and put her hair up in the pink plastic rollers she liked. Most important of all, Maggie did everything she could to make the house safe—unplugging, hiding, locking anything that Edna might hurt herself with. As she hurried now toward the kitchen, though, her mind was stuck on the possibility that she had missed something, some innocent-seeming item that in the hands of a person who was seni . . . who was like her mother could be dangerous. Only when she found the kitchen empty and in order did she exhale.

Maggie headed for the den, where Edna sometimes went for an afternoon "lie down," but as soon as she entered the hallway, she stopped short at the sight of the open front door at the far end. Snowflakes were swirling through it, and a dusting of them had accumulated on the floor. Her attention was next seized by an empty hook on an adjacent wall, where Maggie had hung Edna's gray tweed coat when they came home from nine o'clock Mass that morning.

She tried to check her rising panic with a glance at the clock, which showed that she had slept less than fifteen minutes. No need to worry. Mum couldn't have gotten far in such a short time. She *couldn't* have. And besides, it was such a safe neighborhood—a fabulous neighborhood, right?

Nobody ever got mugged, and there was hardly any traffic.

Maggie's anxiety, like her guilt, was a wily, bullish sort, which quickly dispatched her puny attempt at self-calming with a classic sucker punch: "*Yeah, but if anything did happen, you'd never forgive yourself. Never.*"

Panic surging like a lava flow, Maggie grabbed her jacket and keys and ran out the door.

♦ ♦ ♦

Before Maggie pulled out of the driveway, Edna had progressed at a brisk pace to the end of the street.

"They'll be so happy to see me," she said. "And we can all have this nice snack together."

As she turned the corner, though, the purpose of her excursion—to bring hot-crossed buns to Mutti and Rosamund—disappeared like the light of a snuffed-out candle, and the box of scouring pads in her hand did nothing to rekindle it. Her pace slowed. She was suddenly very tired, and she wanted to go home and have a lie down. The Victorian wonderland she now scanned, though, produced nothing but a frown. Where was Pat Roy's Pharmacy? The Avenue Bakery? Eddie Jack's Market? The Connemara Bar and Grille?

"Hmm . . . I don't think I'm in Dorchester. I wonder how I get back there from here."

Still in possession of the calm resourcefulness that fueled her rise as a union leader, Edna studied her surroundings further, and in a few moments, her face glowed with satisfaction.

"Of course!" she exclaimed. "By bus!"

The vehicle she had caught sight of was a silver-toned Suburban LT, parked in the driveway of Charlie and Rita Costello.

"Oh, I'm so lucky it hasn't left yet!" she said as she climbed into the back seat.

The plush upholstery struck her as a bit fancy-shmancy for the T, but it felt good, very good. With a yawn, she stretched out on it and fell asleep just as Rita stepped out her front door.

8 - Freakin' Epic

Trapped in what his mother used to call a "wicked snit," with WZLX cranked up to drown out the din in the back and further attempts by Mum in his head to cheer him up, Billy scanned the transportation list Joe had given him. His eyebrows rose when he saw that the first three drop-offs were right there in Chestnut Hill. He would have bet that people in a town like this—what in Dorchester was reverentially referred to as a "good area"—had special children only in the top SAT score, three varsity sports, Ivy League, potential seven-figure salary sense.

One social stereotype dashed, he concocted another: that these kids must be a tough pill to swallow for people accustomed to the best of everything.

Billy pulled up in front of the first house, an imposing white colonial on a grassy lot that would take up a third of Ramsey Street. Zip-code boy jumped out and ran into the open arms of a man who was a dead ringer for George Clooney.

"Natchez, Mississippi!" the man called out.

"Easy, Dad! 39120, 39121, 39122!"

"That's my boy! Let's get ready for a run!"

At the next stop, song girl received a similarly warm greeting from a woman with the statuesque figure and flawless face of Nicole Kidman.

"How's Mommy's sweet one?" the woman asked.

"Sweet Ca-ro-line . . ." the girl replied.

"Good times never seemed so g-o-o-d . . ." the mother chimed in.

They walked arm in arm toward the door, harmonizing: "I'd be inclined—oh-oh-oh—to believe they never would . . ."

Billy drove on, the loss of his presumptions serving only to further charge his snit.

He arrived at the third house, expecting another Hollywood clone, but instead found a frumpy older woman, who would not have looked out of place at the Sparkle Laundromat on Dot Ave, waiting at the curb. After introducing herself, peanut boy's grandmother asked Billy, "So where's Joe today?"

The temptation to tell her the truth made Billy smile, but loyalty stifled it even before Mum in his head could ante in.

"Oh, he woke up with a nasty sore throat and didn't want to take the chance of infecting the children—you know, in the close quarters of the van," Billy answered with a look of mock concern that she ate up.

"Isn't that just like Joe?" she asked, shaking her head.

"Isn't it, though?" Billy replied, shaking his.

"Wait here a sec, will you?"

With that, she rushed into the house and soon emerged with a bulging plastic bag.

"Peanut butter cookies—homemade. They're Joe's favorite. Tell him Doreen hopes he feels better soon."

"Peanut butter cookies! Want peanut butter cookies!" Mikey cried

"Of course, Mikey," Doreen replied. "Let's go have some, with tea!"

"Want tea! Want tea!"

At the nearest gas station, Billy got out and threw the bag of cookies into a trash bin. He was on his way to the adjacent convenience store to get a cup of bad coffee when several worst-case scenarios stopped him—one of the kids going psycho on the others or all of them wandering off like the mental patients in that movie, *King of Hearts*. The way his day was going, one or the other was likely.

By the time he had dropped the next kid off at a grimy apartment building overlooking the defunct Allston railyards, his snit was a pulsating force, and this trip, the American Dream in reverse: from the land of tree-lined streets with cute names like Larkspur Lane, where all the houses were way nicer than any funeral home in Dorchester, all the way back to the real world of traffic and litter, sirens and car alarms, panhandlers and punks.

The last stop was only a few blocks from his own house. It was a forlorn three-decker on Columbia Road, stuck between an on-ramp of the Southeast Expressway and an abandoned garage that bore a faded, peeling sign for Frankie's Car Tunes. According to the list, it was the home of Jimmy Garrity, a speechless kid who had smiled and giggled during the entire ride. Nobody was waiting for the boy at the curb, so Billy accompanied him as he limped up the weedy walkway past a rusted, overturned grocery cart and a dead poinsettia still in its red foil wrapper. Halfway to the stoop, Billy saw a man step out onto the porch of the second-floor apartment. He didn't recognize him, but he knew too well the menace in his scowl and the fist clenched around a beer can, and he didn't have to imagine the asshole's appetite for making those he should love miserable. His take on the guy was confirmed when they reached the door, where Jimmy turned toward Billy with fearful, beseeching eyes.

Billy was seized by the urge to grab Jimmy, to get him back into the van, and . . . well, at this point, real-world logic blocked his train of thought. How was he going to save this kid? Bring him home to live with a guy who was as much of a jerk as the one he already lived with? Or maybe grab the Pinto and hit the road to La La Land like Joe and Miranda?

He answered by entering the house with Jimmy and watching from the dark vestibule as the kid climbed the stairs and disappeared into his apartment.

Back in the van, Billy drove off without a glance at the house. He had an hour before he could drop the van off at Vin's, plenty of time to drown his snit in PBR—or maybe Sam Adams, why the hell not? He deserved it after all he'd been through today. He opted for the Tam in Southie over the Connemara. He wouldn't know anybody there, and the thought of being surrounded by nameless old drunks was an oddly comforting one.

A few minutes later, he pulled into the bar's back alley because with his luck, if he parked on the street, somebody who worked for Vin would see the van and report it to the boss. As he was maneuvering into a tight space next to the dumpster, he looked into the rearview mirror, and in that moment, his dream of a peaceful, boozy hour was lost.

The skinny torso of a little boy rose to a sitting position in the back of the van. He yawned, stretched his arms, and looked around. Billy saw and heard all this, but as if he were already drunk, his brain couldn't connect sensory input to rational thought, so overwhelmed was he by the feeling that he was staring at an image of himself in second grade at Saint A's when Mum used to cut his bangs slightly crooked and make him wear a knitted hat with ear flaps and a dangling pom-pom.

"What the . . ." he managed to say.

A few moments later, his current predicament came into focus, whereupon Billy grabbed the transportation list. Before looking at it, though, he closed his eyes and made another attempt to channel some positive energy. The mistake must be his. The snit had distracted him. He'd just missed the kid's name and address on the list. He could rectify it. He could backtrack and tell the parents he'd gotten a flat and his cell phone had died, so he couldn't call them. No biggie. They'd understand. Everybody gets a flat. Everybody's cell phone dies. Everything was going to be okay.

He drew a deep breath, opened his eyes, and scanned the list, only to discover what a crock of shit positive energy was. He had not missed a name. There was no other name, no other address. This kid was going nowhere.

He crumpled the paper into a wad and pounded his fist on the dashboard as if determined to crack it.

"FUCK! FUCK THAT GODDAMN DICKHEAD! I'LL FUCKING RIP OFF HIS BA . . ."

"*BILLY!*" Mum in his head shrieked. "*You sound like your father! And in front of the poor little boy! REMEMBER WHAT IT WAS LIKE?*"

Billy spun around, far more alarmed than the kid, who was watching him with seemingly detached curiosity, the way he might from a safe distance regard a caged lion at the Franklin Park Zoo. Billy saw that except for the bad haircut and funny hat, the kid didn't resemble Billy's younger self at all. He looked more like one of the pink-cheeked shepherd boys pictured on a watercolor Christmas card Billy's mother had framed and put on top of the TV every year. Whether it was the memory of that image, or the eyes of this kid gazing at him—like the shepherd boy's, so wide and clear and calm—Billy was not sure, but something quieted his heaving breath as well as his heart, which had been trying to punch its way out of his chest. The longer he looked at the boy, the more philosophical Billy felt about the same circumstances that just a few moments ago had made him borderline homicidal.

At length, he asked the boy in a quiet tone, "You don't talk, do you?"

After a prolonged silence, Billy answered the question himself: "Of course, you don't."

He pulled out his cell phone to call Joe, knowing from experience that the call would probably go to his friend's voicemail because of a dead battery and that even if he did leave a message, the odds of Joe's responding to it in time were less than those of selling his fridge art. As soon as he speed-dialed the number, Billy heard a ringing inside the van—beneath him, it seemed. He closed his eyes and shook his head as he contemplated a possibility he hadn't even thought of. Then he reached under the seat and pulled out Joe's phone.

"Of course, it's here," he whispered.

He scanned the alley as if some viable option might be hiding there, but he found none. He couldn't call Joe or the kid's family, and calling Saint Theresa's would be throwing Joe under a bus, jobwise, which he didn't want to do, despite the fact that if the guy suddenly appeared, Billy's anger would probably resurge enough to throw him under a real bus.

A ray of hope suddenly appeared in the form of a bread-delivery truck backing onto the loading dock of the variety store next door to the bar. It bore the logo of the bakery that supplied Eddie Jack's. Eddie. If anybody could help Billy, it was Eddie. He was always talking about the scrapes he'd gotten out of, like the time back in high school, when he was in the middle of getting it on with some girl when her father came home. Quick as a firefighter, Eddie jumped out her bedroom window with his shoes, pants, and jacket in his arms and landed in a snowbank two stories down, where he wriggled into his clothes and then sauntered off whistling. Or the time his buddy O'Hara was driving them home from Cape Cod and got stopped in Neponset for speeding. Figuring the cop was Irish, Eddie said to O'Hara, "Follow my lead," and once the guy was within earshot, shouted at his friend: "You fuckin' stupid Harp! I told you to slow down! But you were too fired up to get to some gin mill and park your dumb Irish ass on a barstool, weren't you?" The cop shot Eddie a look hot with ethnic outrage and then let O'Hara off with nothing more than the admonition to get a new friend. Eddie's skills—not just channeling positive energy but doing it in a sprint—were just what Billy needed.

He glanced back at the kid. Maybe he had those skills, too—why else would he be so tranquil, stuck in a weird place with a strange guy who swore and yelled? On the chance that he might catch more of these vibes if the kid were closer, Billy jumped out and led him to the front seat. By the time he had buckled him in, the absurdity of this logic hit Billy like a slush ball in the face.

"Christ, I've lost it," he said, turning toward the boy, and with a hand on his shoulder added, "And you, kid? You're lost. We got our own *Odyssey* going here. We're freakin' epic."

The boy blinked his watercolor-shepherd boy's eyes at him and settled back in the seat as if it were a massage chair. Billy cleared his throat and drove off.

9 - Oops.

Marie Cagianelli sat at her desk in the office at Saint Theresa's, her eyes closed, her breath slow and rhythmic. Her hands rested on her lap, palms up with her thumbs and index fingers gently touching. She, too, was trying to channel positive energy. More accurately, the channel she was seeking was her recently deceased husband, Dom. When he was alive—here on earth, that is—the two of them always made important decisions together: whether to send the kids to public or parochial school, to get replacement windows or a new roof, to celebrate their twenty-fifth anniversary with a long weekend in New York or a full week on the Cape, and they had valued and relied on each other's take on things. Now Marie was facing a big decision by herself, and she felt her loss—no, not loss, her physical separation—as acutely as the back spasms she developed during Dom's chemotherapy. Joe Doherty, whom she had often confided in since Dom's death—passing, rather—because he had such a sympathetic ear and a lot of wisdom for somebody so young, told her that what she was feeling was essentially a swell of negative energy that she could dispel with its opposite force, just like he did with his artwork. He admitted to her that he had lots of doubts and fears about making it as a professional, but that the more he doubted himself, the more he kept on painting. He was literally turning his anxieties into art, which he had read most creative people do.

On his recommendation, Marie had consulted websites on positive channeling, which listed the "Top Ten" or the "Three Essential" or the "Twenty Basic" steps to doing it successfully. She tried recognizing her own power, using words that evoked strength and success, creatively visualizing, filtering out doubt, and silently repeating an upbeat mantra. She alternated between *The sun will come out tomorrow* and *I will survive*, lyrics from two of her favorite songs.

Despite her most earnest effort, though, none of the techniques dispelled her negative energy, leaving her as discouraged as she had been after her last diet-and-exercise regimen, which, after four months, resulted in the loss of only two pounds.

Once Marie realized how much she stunk at solo positive channeling, her longing for Dom, which she had been squelching because she read in a self-help book that once you go down that road, you can get lost, exploded inside her like a bad case of acid reflux, and sure enough, she felt lost. Then, in the middle of Sunday mass a few weeks ago, she felt a profound truth that her negative energy had hidden: since our souls were immortal, Dom was still alive, and since he was still alive, she could still turn to him, and he could be in on the decision—not the way he would be here on earth, but spiritually through *his* positive energy, which, she supposed, somebody in heaven must have tons of. With renewed hope, she had been trying to reach him ever since, even at work when Sister Esther wasn't around to catch her in what looked like a trance, but she still hadn't heard from him. Of course, she didn't expect him to speak from the clouds with one of his classic encouragements—*Go for broke, Marie!*—but she was hoping for some kind of sign that would inspire her with the confidence to make the right choice.

Her problem was that her friend Donna was opening a beauty parlor and had offered Marie a job. At first, the opportunity seemed like a dream come true, because it was just the kind of work Marie had trained for right after high school when she was a newlywed with dreams of opening her own shop someday. Even before she finished beauty school, she had picked a name for it, *Salon Magique,* because it had a classy, continental sound to it, and because, really, what woman didn't want her hairdresser to work magic? But ten months after her wedding, along came a set of twins, Dom Jr. and Johnny and a year later, another, Tony and Peter. She had hoped to return to hairstyling once the kids were in school, but when the time came, she and Dom agreed that the office job at Saint Theresa's was a more sensible and responsible choice because of the family-friendly hours and benefits, and of course, they wanted to be sensible and responsible parents.

But now the boys were all grown up and off on their own, and Dom was gone, too—to his eternal reward, of course—and Marie wanted to *live in the moment*, as Joe called "doing what you feel you need to right now to be happy and fulfilled and not letting yourself be inhibited by what-ifs and practical considerations." The pressing part of the situation was that Donna needed to know by the following week whether or not Marie was going to take the job, which she really wanted, but it was super hard, after all those years of being sensible and responsible, to make such a radical change. She was totally sick of the same old typing and filing and kowtowing to persnickety Sister Esther's "office protocols," but they were familiar and safe, and well, maybe she needed familiar and safe in her life right now. Or maybe that was just negative energy talking.

Marie jumped when the phone rang, thinking for one crazy moment that Dom was calling her with advice.

"If only," she whispered with a sigh before she picked up the phone.

"Saint Theresa's," she said in the bright, welcoming, and totally automatic tone she had greeted callers with for thirty years.

"Hey, Marie—Wil Dodge."

"Hi, Wi . . ."

"Listen, change of plans, I can't pick Robby up today. Something's come up, so make sure he gets in the van, okay? Maggie knows about it, so it's covered on the home end."

"Sure, no probl . . ."

"Great. Listen, gotta run. Thanks."

Marie hung up and shook her head. What did a sweetheart like Maggie see in a guy who was so full of himself that he probably didn't even need to eat? How lucky Marie had been—still was—to be married to someone as generous and kind as Dom! As she stared out the window, contemplating her blessing, she suddenly saw Joe shepherding the kids into the van. Her attempts at positive channeling had caused her to lose track of time. She jumped up from her chair, dashed into the hallway, sprinted to Robby's classroom, and with a quick explanation to his teacher, grabbed the boy and his jacket. By the time they reached the parking lot, Joe was at the far end about to pull out onto the street, but Marie's waving arm managed to catch his attention, and he backed up.

"One more for the road?" he asked, revealing that adorable smile of his. It struck her for the first time how similar Joe's adorable smile was to Dom's—boyish and sincere and with just a hint of dimples. She watched Joe buckle Robby into a seat in the back row and listened to him chat with the boy with the same gentle, good-natured humor that Dom used to show their kids. And then, when Joe was behind the wheel again, he rolled down the window and said it.

"I'm glad this happened, Marie, because well, I don't know why, but I've been thinking about you a lot today—you know, your big decision and everything—and, well, I just want to tell you . . ."

Unlike most men, who just didn't understand that women liked eye contact, *needed* eye contact, Joe was looking directly at her, just the way Dom used to. Oh, how Marie missed the heart-to-heart and eye-to-eye talks she and her wonderful husband had! With Dom's gaze fixed on her, she always knew that they weren't just discussing this or that, but really *communicating*. And now, strangely, she had that old, familiar certainty. It was as if Dom were with her again. She felt her face flush and her heartbeat, which just had recovered from all the running, resurge.

"And, well, I say, *Go for broke, Marie!*" Joe declared.

After Joe had driven off, Marie walked—no, *floated*—back to the office. She called Donna with the news that she was going to take the leap, and they made plans to celebrate with drinks after work. When Sister Esther returned from an off-campus meeting, Marie gave her two weeks' notice and got in return a frown and a judgmental "Well, if that type of thing appeals to you, dear." Talk about negative energy! Marie deftly countered it, though, with a smile that felt delicious.

It wasn't until she was in the car on her way to meet Donna that she remembered that the day's transportation list she had given Joe that morning wasn't accurate because it didn't include Robby's information. At first, she was a little panicky at having broken one of Sister Esther's beloved protocols, which, although she thought most of them were completely OCD and a stupid waste of time, Marie had always followed. The fear was banished, though, by her yummy smile, which a quick look in the rearview mirror showed was also radiant.

Basking in positive energy, Marie said out loud, "What difference does the list make anyway? It's not like Joe doesn't know where Robby lives."

10 - Q and A

Stretched out on the bed in his room at the Econo-Rest Motor Lodge on Morrissey Boulevard in Dorchester, Eamon Lally munched cheese curls and watched his baseball career unfold in a succession of twenty-second clips on a cheap flat-screen TV that was bolted to the wall above a dresser with chipped faux wood veneer and a missing drawer. Bert Altmeier, a WBZ sportscaster, was narrating the report, which the title in the upper right corner of the screen identified as "Boston's Most Wanted."

The first shot showed Eamon with his team at Bishop Brandt High School in West Milwaukee after they had won the state baseball championship his freshman year. Adult Eamon observed that his teenage self was the only one not smiling giddily, the only one not smiling at all, in fact, and that he looked confused by all the jubilation around him. Of course, he had understood back then that winning the states was "mega-huge," in Coach Rachaelski's often repeated words, and he was glad the team had done it, but he hadn't known how much less glad he was than everyone else until it happened. He liked baseball well enough because it was a fun game that he had gotten pretty good at—well, probably better than pretty good. It was just a game, though, like a math test was just a math test.

"*Bishop Brandt won the states all four years Lally pitched for them,*" Altmeier said, in a solemn tone, "*and each year he won the MVP award, an astounding record that may never be broken.*"

Next came a video of nineteen-year-old Eamon holding up a Red Sox jersey while he stood between the team's general manager, Steve Theobald and the owner, Henley Johnson. Both men were flashing broad, toothy, gleaming smiles. With pursed lips and darting eyes, Eamon looked as if he was searching for the closest exit, which, he now recalled, was sort of what he had been doing. He liked Mr. Theobald and Mr. Johnson, and Mr. Buck, his agent, but it bothered him that each one had told him "in strict confidence" that he was the answer to their prayers, because, well, he couldn't think of himself that way. Prayers were to keep people safe and healthy, or to help get them into heaven when they died. Winning baseball games just didn't seem as important, but he didn't tell them that because he couldn't stand disappointing people.

"*The Red Sox brass nabbed Lally in the first round of the draft, pinning on him their hopes of finally reversing The Curse,*" Altmeier said, drawing out the last three words.

Eamon's throat caught as he tried to swallow a cheese curl.

He was relieved when the report flipped to another image, one that showed him on the mound at McCoy Stadium, in Pawtucket, Rhode Island, home of the Red Sox AAA affiliate, where he had spent the first three months of his rookie year. As he was every time he saw films of himself, Eamon was struck by his windup and delivery. They looked weird. Really, really weird, as if a big, floppy puppet controlled by the invisible strings of some crazy drunk guy were throwing the ball. His right arm whipped backward so far and his left leg jerked upward so high that it seemed that he was going to keel over and land on his butt. At that pivotal moment, though, the arm reversed direction in a sideways-ish arc—if anything so erratic could be called an arc—while the right leg stretched backward until the knee almost touched the mound and the left foot returned to earth to brace the lunging torso, and in the midst of all this freaky yoga movement, the ball was projected at bullet-speed toward the batter, who, if he was super lucky, might get a decent piece of it.

To be honest, Eamon was still as mystified by his pitch as everyone else and had been since his family came to the US from Ireland and a neighbor told his mother that there was nothing more American than baseball. She signed him up for Little League tryouts as soon as he was old enough because she wanted him to fit in with the other lads, which, up to that point, his shyness had kept him from doing.

When his earliest coaches saw how he threw, they all laughed and asked him, "Did ya learn that back in the old country, boyo?" They tried to teach him to pitch with "better economy" and "more flow" and "less awkwardness," by which Eamon figured they meant *more normally*. But once they noticed how well his style worked, how it messed with every lesson that had been drilled into batters about "getting a read on the ball"—one coach described the pitch as "hieroglyphics in motion"—they encouraged Eamon to go on pitching his own way, which was good because every attempt he had made to do it normally had been pretty much a disaster.

"With the Pawsox, Lally's inexplicable, inimitable, indomitable style brought him six wins in six starts and a phenomenal ERA of 1.90." Altmeier put melodramatic emphasis on each adjective.

The next clip, shot a few months after Eamon had been called up to Boston, showed his teammates swarming him after the final out of a no-hitter against the Yankees in New York. They were jumping up and down like little kids on a trampoline, their delight unrestrained, giddy even. Eamon watched himself being swept up and carried to the dugout and felt now what he'd felt then—embarrassed. He knew that what he had accomplished was a big deal to everyone in the farthest reaches of "Red Sox Nation," especially because it happened towards the end of a pennant race. He had seen the "Yankees Suck" t-shirts and had heard the "Evil Empire" moniker and the painful legend of Bucky Dent. But even though he'd much rather win than lose, it felt kind of crazy for everyone to act as if he were a war hero or something. He didn't save his platoon by defusing a bomb or rescue a buddy by carrying him on his back through the jungle. He just won a ballgame! Now he watched the scene shift to the clubhouse, where a dozen reporters shoved microphones at him and asked for his thoughts, and he heard himself say, "Well, I guess I just did my job."

The TV screen flashed back to the studio, and Eamon saw Altmeier sitting behind the broadcast desk. His lips were pressed together, as if he were trying to hold back tears, and his head was shaking ever so slightly.

"'I guess I just did my job,'" he said. *"What a modest genius. But now . . . a missing one, too."*

As Eamon reached for the remote, he heard Altmeier speaking to him.

"And if you're listening, Eamon . . . come home. We want you, and we need you."

If Eamon could have responded, he would have said, "You're sure not making this any easier, Mr. Altmeier."

Instead, he clicked the set off, stepped to the window, and looked out at the heavy gray clouds over Dorchester Bay. They reminded him of County Cork, except for the snow they were spewing. Back home, it would have been rain. He hadn't missed home in a long time, especially the rain, but now he did. He wouldn't be in this fix if his family had just stayed there. Nobody in County Cork played baseball.

Even more than he longed for the old country, Eamon yearned for a decent meal. During his two days at the Econo-Rest, he had been subsisting on vending machine food—peanut butter crackers, granola bars, licorice drops, and cheese curls, which, if he didn't think about the neon-orange color, were strangely comforting. Still, he was dying to go to a restaurant, maybe the Papa Gino's across the street, or just to the 7-Eleven next door for some sandwich fixings. If he did, though, he might be recognized, and somebody might report having seen him. Then he'd be found, and even more than he wanted real food, Eamon wanted not to be found. He wanted to think, and hopefully to find an answer to a question he'd been avoiding for a long time. And to do that he had to be lost.

He hadn't really *decided* to be lost; it was a spur-of-the-moment idea that struck him as he was driving from the airport to his condo in Quincy after the team had returned from Florida. He simply got off the Southeast Expressway at Neponset Circle and ended up here. Luckily, the check-in clerk, Aroosh, according to his name tag, didn't seem to recognize his face. Just to be safe, Eamon signed into the room with his father's first name and his mother's maiden name and paid for three nights in cash. As soon as he got to his room, he called his parents to tell them where he was and why. He didn't tell them exactly what the question was—maybe he was still avoiding it a little—just that he had to make a decision about his career. They didn't press him about it, though. His dad said he was a level-headed lad and that he'd figure it out, whatever it was. His mum, who he suspected knew what was on his mind simply because she always did, told him that he would find his true self if he trusted his heart.

"And then, love," she said, "you'll have no choice."

They both pledged to say the rosary for him every day and to love him "always, all ways." After Eamon had hung up the phone, he cried.

Since then, he had tried putting the question into words on paper because his mum always told him that some thoughts—worries, for instance—you just can't properly deal with in your head, that you've got to see them. The results were written on pieces of Econo-Rest note paper: *What do I want from life? What would make me happy? What am I meant to be? What's wrong?*

His satisfaction at seeing the questions was quickly followed by the realization that now he was supposed to answer them. He didn't feel quite up to the task, so he kept adding questions because that meant he was at least working on the problem: *What are my goals? What's important to me? How do I want to be remembered?*

At last count, the list numbered forty-two, but that seemed a bit much, so he tried to put them into categories and pick the best ones from each, a "winnowing" technique that his senior-year English teacher Sister Paulette Anthony had taught as a way of writing essays that were "clear and concise." Eamon never had much success with winnowing in high school—the words "rambling" and "repetitive" appeared in red ink in the margins of most of the essays Sister returned to him—and today after an hour and a half of struggling, he discovered that he still pretty much sucked at it. It also occurred to him that maybe he was avoiding answering the questions as much as he had avoided asking them. That was the point when he turned on the TV.

Now Eamon turned away from the window and fished *Inspiring Lives* out of his duffle on the floor. Sitting at the desk, he reread some of his old favorites but found that the super dramatic sacrifices of the martyrs were not moving him as they usually did. He turned instead to stories he had glossed over before, stories about men and women who hadn't died for their faith but had kept on living for it: Saint Margaret of Lorraine, a widowed duchess, who could have spent all her money on clothes and jewels but instead built convents, schools, and churches and protected peasants from greedy landlords; Saint Cuthbert, a shepherd boy who became a monk when he was only fifteen and during a pestilence used his cheerful personality to convince people not to get scared back into their pagan ways; Saint Monica, whose prayers resulted in her cheating, pagan husband becoming a devout Catholic and her party-boy son, Augustine, a saint; and Saint Francis, who after his rich, stuck-up father disinherited him for helping poor and sick people, begged on the streets for money and helped them anyway.

After more than an hour, Eamon closed the book. When he raised his head, he saw the reflection of his face split in two by a crack in the mirror, and he turned away from it when he saw how troubled he looked. Then he remembered what Diego Ortega had once told him about mindfulness meditation—that if you looked hard at something right in front of you, but didn't think about it or about anything else, you could "center" yourself, which would calm you down and help you see things more clearly.

Well, that's just what Eamon needed now, so he turned his head back to the mirror and focused on his eyes, straining to hold the gaze and to block out everything else. For the first few minutes it was hard—he had never been much for looking at himself—and his mind was still teaming with questions and saints. After a while, though, the strain lessened. His neck and jaw relaxed, his breathing quieted, and most significantly, his eyes brightened. When he finally broke his focus on them, his smile appeared. It just flickered at first, but soon it illuminated his whole face. And he was still looking at it as he picked up the phone to call directory assistance, marveling at what you could find in a mirror.

11 - Shedding

Maggie watched two uniformed policemen walk back to the squad car parked in her driveway. A cluster of worry lines appeared on her forehead as she recalled how the older one, Officer Preston, who had done the questioning, either raised or lowered his eyebrows at some of her responses. They were like two dark, bushy caterpillars, impossible to ignore, and each time they moved, Maggie's heart sank. Were they revealing skepticism? Shock? Disapproval? Now, as she saw him looking at the photo that she had given him a few minutes earlier, she second guessed her choice, one of Edna at the dining room table, smiling over a bowl of oyster stew last Christmas Eve. Maybe Maggie should have found one of her mother's looking anxious or confused, like the kind of old person who would wander off after her daughter fell asleep. Edna always smiled for a camera, though, and besides, Officer Preston seemed satisfied with it—at least his eyebrows didn't move when he looked at it.

Maggie smiled as she saw his partner, Officer Lee, pocketing the notebook he had recorded her responses in. While she was speaking, she felt that his gentle brown eyes—they reminded her of Sweety's—conveyed understanding and sympathy, but now she wondered if it had just been pity for someone so stupid that she couldn't keep tabs on one old lady.

Answering some of the questions had made Maggie feel a little less guilty. Yes, Edna was wearing an identification bracelet with her home address and phone number engraved on it. (Maggie had gotten one of these after seeing a TV advertisement.) Some, though, felt like stab wounds. No, she had not alerted all the neighbors to her mother's condition—a few people at church knew—but it just seemed kind of a private thing. (After this response, Officer Preston's eyebrows plummeted so low that they converged at the bridge of his nose.) Maggie was comforted by Officer Lee's assertion that elderly people like Edna were often found soon after wandering off. Maybe she had slipped into someone's house, and when they found her asleep on their bed and read her bracelet, they would bring her right home. Then she panicked when Officer Preston said that in cases of dementia—she wasn't surprised that he used that word—the missing person sometimes tried to return to a former residence or workplace. What if Edna stumbled upon the T station off Hammond Street and some sympathetic person gave her money for the fare? She could be wandering anywhere in Boston looking for City Hall Plaza or Bay View Street!

After the officers had driven off, Maggie went to the kitchen to do what she always did when she needed to steady herself—make soup. She took three hefty Yukon Golds from a drawer and started scrubbing them at the sink in preparation for Edna's favorite, cream of potato (secret ingredient: the skins). For once, though, her faithful, therapeutic routine couldn't subdue her troubled mind, which was whirling with images of her mother being hit by a truck on Dot Ave, her lifeless body lying in a litter-strewn gutter, or of her slipping on the icy steps in the cavernous brick expanse of City Hall Plaza, writhing in pain from a broken hip.

Maggie suddenly remembered the last—no, she thought, not the last, the *most recent*—conversation she'd had with Edna, when her mother insisted that the garden shed was her old office building. The possibility that Edna might be there, asleep in the lawn chair that Maggie had brought in from the yard so her mother could watch her when she potted plants for the deck, set Maggie's heart racing.

"Don't get your hopes up, Maggie," she said out loud, but she rushed out the kitchen door as if Edna were calling her.

She repeated the command all the way across the slushy grass; nonetheless, by the time she'd reached the shed, her hopes were like kites whirling in a clear blue sky. They crashed, though, as soon as she entered. In the dim afternoon light, she saw clay pots stacked on shelves, sacks of fertilizer in bins on the floor, hand tools hanging from wall hooks, and a mouse nest in a corner beneath the counter. But the lawn chair was empty.

"I'm sorry, Mum," Maggie whispered, as she stared at it. "I didn't take care of you."

Maggie rarely cried. She loved her father dearly. He had been more like an older brother, really, or a best friend, someone you turned to when you didn't know how you felt, and then after talking to him, you did. And yet, she remained dry eyed when she learned that he had been killed in a hit-and-run at Upham's Corner, dry eyed during the two-day wake at Minehan's Funeral Home, dry eyed at the burial in Holy Cross Cemetery. A day after the funeral, though, and for most of the next month, she had a recurring dream: she was sitting at a table in an otherwise empty room with a dessert in front of her—one night, chocolate cake; the next, pumpkin pie; on subsequent nights, cookies or tarts or eclairs. Maggie looked at them longingly, knowing who had made them for her, but she didn't touch them. She only cried. It was always a downpour of tears, furious and unremitting, accompanied by wailing and groaning that sounded as if she were trying to expel her heart through her mouth. Each morning when she woke up, she remembered the dream, but her eyes remained dry. Not long after that dream had stopped, the Sweety Dreams as she now knew them began, often veiled but always timely, and they ultimately encouraged her to believe, with a faith that Catholicism had never come close to inspiring, that her father was still alive and with her, just in a different way.

As she stood now in the shed, Maggie sobbed quietly, and as she did, the anxiety and remorse that had been pressing on her for the past two hours subsided a little.

"I didn't take care of you, Mum," she repeated. "But Sweety will."

12 - Saint Frank

At the seminary gate, Wil found Richie Buck, whose slick black hair and matching leather jacket were flaked with snow like a hideous case of dandruff. Cell phone pressed to his ear, he popped pink balloons of bubble gum, which he once told Wil was a "piss fuckin' poor" replacement for the cigarettes his doctor had predicted would kill him, and by extension, his dream of representing a potential Hall-of-Famer. The scowl he now shot at Wil showed just how unhappy he was that his only such prospect in ten years was on the verge of dumping him "for fuckin' sackcloth and ashes."

By way of greeting, Richie snapped the phone shut and barked, "Okay, Dodgeball, here's what ya do—go in there and TALK HIM THE FUCK OUT OF IT!"

Pop!

This was only the first explosion of gum and of words. After each one that followed, Richie's mouth sucked in the deflated remains of the bubble and produced another with barely a pause.

"This kid's stock's goin' back up, I tell ya—WAY UP!"

Pop!

"And I got a lot a lot INVESTED in him!"

Pop!

"But I get DIDDLY if he quits to go bless BABIES AND STIFFS!"

Pop!

"So, whatever your angle is, get in there and understand him back to the FUCKIN' BALLPARK!"

Pop!

Wil had never witnessed Richie in "full exclamatory mode," but Jimmy Higgins in the Red Sox GM's office, who had coined the phrase, once told him there was no use reasoning with the guy when he was in it: "You might as well try to put out a five-alarmer with a squirt gun."

Thus forewarned, Wil simply nodded and walked up the path to the main door. When he reached it, he heard Richie barking the same marching order Barney Killian had given an hour earlier.

"MAKE IT HAPPEN, Dodgeball!"

Wil entered a large, dimly lit foyer, its oak-paneled walls bearing so much Catholic iconography that the game face Wil had assumed started to crack. He used to get a big kick out of the adorational symbols of Catholics, like the little shrine to the Blessed Mother the Joyces had in their postage stamp of a front yard. The three-foot statue stood in an upended, half-sunken bathtub painted sky blue and decorated with plastic roses. What a hoot! Ditto Edna's collection of Infant of Prague figurines, one in every room—including the bath—of her old apartment in Dot. Now he eyed the array with the same holy-shit look he had worn as a ten-year-old when a scrum of bigger kids was barreling toward him on the playground during games of kill-the-guy-with-the ball, and he felt similarly unnerved. To regain his bravado, he walked right up to a painting of a bearded, haloed man in a brown robe and sandals, the least intimidating image of the lot. He stepped closer and read the gold plate at the base of the frame: Saint Francis of Assisi.

"Saint Frank himself," Wil said, rolling his eyes. Almost immediately, his grin faded as a creepy sensation struck—that Saint Frank was looking back at him, looking *through* him, really, and feeling . . . disappointed.

Wil turned away, but his gaze landed on a bronze plaque engraved with a prayer:

O Lord, grant that I might not so much seek to be helped, as to help;

To be understood, as to understand.

For it is in giving that we receive.

Wil looked up again at the saintly visage and said with as much cockiness as he could summon, "But it is in *winning* that we win, Frank."

The holy man remained silent, but his dark eyes bored deeper into Wil, with mesmerizing effect. Finally, he cleared his throat and rushed off to find the rector's office, trying to reset his game face. Something had started gnawing at him, though, and he didn't know what it was. Maybe just nerves or . . . then he recognized the feeling he'd gotten the last time he let Lally go on about martyrs—compassion! Saint Frank's freakin' eyes made him go soft and fuzzy!

Not now, Wil, he thought. *NOT NOW. Shake it off, for Chrissake*!

He found this command hard to follow as he strode down the hall because, unless he closed his eyes, he could not escape the gauntlet of Sacred Hearts, Virgin Mothers—and, of course, saints and martyrs—that were looking down on him, literally and maybe figuratively, from their frames on the walls. At last, he came upon a door with a frosted-glass window bearing the name *Monsignor Raymond P. Canny, Rector*, and he gripped the knob, bracing himself for another onslaught of holy images.

When Wil opened the door, though, his face brightened at the sight of autographed photos of the Red Sox, Celtics, Bruins, and Patriots. He was further cheered by a framed poster that depicted a brawny farmer, his shirtsleeves pushed above his elbows, pulling a cart with a bull at the reins. The caption read: *Guinness for Strength.*

"Hi, there."

The greeter was a trim guy not much older than Wil, wearing jeans and a short-sleeved black shirt with a Roman collar. He was on the top rung of a ladder, struggling to pry loose the globe of a ceiling lamp. Wil recalled the setup of an old Lovey Joyce joke: "How many priests does it take to change a light bulb?" The punch line eluded him, though.

"Boss got ya doin' maintenance, eh, padre?"

The priest shot him a thin smile. "Yeah, something like that," he replied.

"Gotta keep the man happy, right?"

"Um . . . right."

"Anyway, I'm Wil Dodge," Wil told him, watching for a sign of recognition that didn't come. "I'm here to talk with Eamon Lally. Richie Buck had made an appointment for me with the monsignor."

The priest, pointing with a screwdriver said, "Eamon's in the conference room," and then returned to the light fixture. "Monsignor Canny will be there in a few minutes. He's just finishing a little project."

Irked that he still couldn't remember the punch line, Wil lingered a few moments before going inside.

There he found Eamon, sitting at a polished, oversized table, head bowed, fingering rosary beads. As if this sight were not discouraging enough, on a pedestal in the corner directly behind the renegade pitcher loomed a large, painted figurine—Saint Frank again! But now his penetrating look was accompanied by a maddeningly serene voice resonating in Wil's head. "O Lord, grant that I might . . ."

Wil tried to drown it out by addressing Eamon. "So, I hear you might be switching teams, kiddo."

But for Wil, there was no escaping maddeningly serene voices, for in just such a tone Eamon replied, "Well . . . I'm thinking about it real hard, Wil."

Channeling Richie's uber angst, Wil was on the verge of shouting, "That's NUTS! FUCKIN'

NUTS!"

But under the more measured influence of Saint Frank, what came out—in a serene, if forced, tone—was, "That's . . . surprising."

"Yeah," agreed Eamon, "I guess it must seem that way to you. But it's been rattling around in the back of my mind a while now; I just didn't know what it was. That's probably why I stunk up the joint so bad last season. My head was outta whack."

"I wish you'd told me. I could have . . . helped." Wil's voice quavered on the last word because he was sure Saint Frank was rolling his eyes.

"Well, actually you did help," Eamon replied. "Y'know that piece you wrote back in September when everybody in town was so down on me? The one where you stood by me? I'll always remember the last two lines, 'He'll dig deep. He'll find his way.' It . . . inspired me, I guess you could say, to think about what's really inside me and what I should be doing with it."

"Damn! DAMN! DAMN! DAMN!" Richie-through-Wil wanted to scream. But again, the holy man in the corner won out. "That's . . . heavy stuff."

"It sure is," Eamon said. "I mean, when everybody's told you that you were meant to do one thing and you do it pretty good—okay, better than pretty good—it's tough to give it up, even if you think the Lord might be calling you."

Inside Wil's head, Richie was screaming, "Then DON'T give it up! Play HARDBALL, kid! KO the Lord back to the HOLY LAND!" What came out of Wil's mouth was "That's quite a choice."

"Yeah, and I've been maybe kind of . . . scared, I guess, to even think about it. So, I really gave it my best shot in camp this spring. I was hoping that'd set me back to normal. But when it was over, I still didn't feel right, and I knew I needed to think on it, which is why I've been

AWOL, I guess you'd say. It just started to come clear to me today, so I called the monsignor for advice—you know, the spiritual kind—because I met him on Clergy Day at Fenway last May, and he seemed like such a kind, wise man. Then before I got here, Richie found me and started pressing—you know how he gets—so I tried to calm him down by telling him I'd talk to you because of all people, you might be the one to . . ."

"Understand," Eamon and Saint Frank in Wil's head chimed in chorus.

"Yeah . . . well . . . I . . ."

Wil was at a loss for words. It didn't happen often, but whenever it did, it shook him. He heard a voice, which, for a

Twilight Zone-ish moment, he thought was Saint Frank's, turned chummy.

"How's it goin', guys?"

"Oh, real good, Monsignor," Eamon replied, standing. "I've been telling Wil here the whole story. I should have called him before, but . . . I don't know. I just felt like keeping to myself."

"Well, blessed be the introverted, Eamon," the monsignor replied. "I'm one myself!"

Wil turned around. The light bulb changer was in the doorway.

"*You're* . . . ?"

"Yeah, it's true, amigo," Monsignor Canny said with a laugh. "I'm 'the man.' And right now, I say it's time for all of us to continue this search for the inner Eamon at the Gardens."

"What's that—some kind of shrine?" Wil, sick to death of Catholicism, asked with a grimace.

"No, no, the Connemara Gardens Bar and Grille. We'll seek divine guidance over a few beers."

"You can . . . do that?" Eamon asked.

"Sure. Remember, the Lord Himself was no teetotaler."

As they put on their coats, Wil asked the priest, "This may seem like a strange question, Father, but where are your parents from?"

"My mother is from County Mayo, and my father's from Dublin. Why?"

"Just curious," Wil answered flatly.

"Now I've got a question for you," the monsignor countered. "How many priests does it take to screw in a light bulb?"

13 - Visions

"And I always thought you were smart," Eddie said.

He removed his rumpled fedora, rubbed his bony fingers through what was left of his gray hair, and shook his head.

"Yeah, well . . . now you know," Billy replied, diverting his eyes to a box of raspberry Danish on the counter. He couldn't remember if he'd ever seen Eddie without the hat, but even if he had, the sight of that blotchy, bone-pale scalp was creeping him out, almost as if the guy had just stripped naked.

"Well, since you're not, let me point out that the parents are gonna be missin' this one pretty damn soon," Eddie said with a nod toward Robby, who was sitting on the freezer case surveying the room with wide eyes more common at fireworks displays than in old, dimly lit grocery stores. "And when they do, it won't be long before the cops get called. They'll get a description of you from those other parents you met on the route, and before you know it, you'll be in the Suffolk County slammer. *Ergo . . .*" He paused to give due emphasis to his *Jeopardy*-acquired Latin. "Ya might as well call the cops yourself and plead stupid."

"I can't. I mean . . . I can, but what about Joe?"

"I keep expectin' him to start oooin' and aaahin'," Eddie observed with another look at

Robby. "He must see somethin' in here we don't. Jeez . . . and they call that a handicap."

With that, he put his hat back on and looked around his humble little establishment as if something grand might appear to him, too.

"Earth to Eddie. I'm waiting."

Billy was usually more patient when Eddie drifted off topic, but now all he wanted was to get out of the trap he was in and have a beer. Still, he was relieved that the hat was back on.

"Right. Pardon the . . . *non sequitur.* Okay, look . . . Joe's a decent guy, Billy—a space-cadet, but a decent guy. And I understand you wantin' to help him, especially after what he did for you way back when. But haven't ya figured out he's gonna catch heat even if ya don't report havin' the kid? The way I see it playin' out is the parents are gonna call Sister Excruciata, or whatever the hell her name is, if they haven't done it already. Then she's gonna call van man and Mrs. Doherty. They'll know diddly squat about what's going on, but they'll be pissed as hell that he bagged another day of work. So as soon as Joe gets his keister back to town, it's gonna get spanked, fired, and kicked outta the house."

"Actually, I . . . I hadn't thought about . . . all that."

"Well, think about it now."

"So, Joe gets screwed no matter what I do."

"I hate to break it to ya, kiddo, but this ain't your shot at playin' payback hero."

Billy's color rose to an indignant red, and the veins at his temples bulged. His eyes fired at the old man while his hard-set mouth opened, ready with an attack he would have regretted.

"*Billy*," Mum in his head, silent for some time now, said.

His anger deflated with a quiet, cheek-bulging sigh, maybe because of her gentle tone or Eddie's hangdog expression. Or maybe Billy was just too honest to argue against the truth, which was that he did feel he owed Joe, big time, and he didn't like the feeling. It wasn't that being grateful bothered him. He was just sick of looking up to Joe, and not just for what he had done on one particular day. It was also for having the guts to keep trying, no matter what, unlike Billy, who just gave up—the way he had one night ten years ago, about a month after Betty Nee's death.

Without the restraining influence of his wife, Leo had already ramped up his abusiveness toward his son. The random whacks he had long inflicted on Billy became harder and more frequent. Still of a slight build at fifteen, Billy ached for hours and was bruised for days after some of the harsher blows. The old outrage he used to feel at his father's mistreatment of him, though, had finally succumbed. He told no one about his injuries, not even Joe, and he imagined no revenge. All he imagined was his mother, resting in peace among other angels, and he longed to be with her.

It was a warm evening in early September. Leo was slouched in a dingy plastic beach chair on the back porch of their first-floor apartment, an empty Styrofoam cooler and the crushed aluminum remains of two six-packs strewn on the floor. Over the din of his favorite radio talk show, whose acerbic host was bashing a caller who had dared to speak against corporal punishment, Leo bellowed, "Gemme more beeeeeer out heeeeere!"

Billy appeared, empty handed, and quietly announced, "None left."

Leo's fuse, short on a good day, was lit.

"Ya little goddamn motherfucker! Whynja tell me we was low!"

An almost imperceptible shrug of Billy's shoulders was all the further provocation his father needed. Leo exploded out of the chair, slammed Billy against the wooden railing, and commenced a beating that might have resulted in serious injury if Joe had not, at the same moment, stepped onto the top-floor porch of his neighboring three-decker. Had Billy looked up, he would have seen his friend standing motionless, his mouth hanging open, as if stunned, not just by Leo's violence, but by Billy's passiveness. As he later told Billy, "Man, you were just standing there, taking it like you had it coming."

A few minutes later, Billy did see Joe burst onto the Nees' porch and grab Leo's arm from behind. Freed from the attack, Billy slid down the railing to the floor, where he sat panting, back slumped and head hung between his bent legs. Only when he heard a pained, guttural sound, did he look up. Joe was still behind Leo, twisting his arm backward and jerking it as he asked, "Want more, Leo? Want more?" Leo's eyes were squeezed shut, and his groans got so loud that Billy had a freakish vision of the arm snapping off and falling to the floor right next to him.

Then Joe swung Leo around and looked down on him from his towering height with a glare that even Billy shrank from.

"You ever—*ever*—so much as touch him again, Leo," he said, Dirty Harry rage in his voice, "I will goddamn *break* you."

Leo's eyes were wide open now. He nodded and kept nodding but said nothing.

Billy had never seen his father look scared, and it struck him that a sixteen-year-old, even a brawny one like Joe, had so clearly terrified the man. It surprised Billy, too, that Leo appeared to stay terrified, because from that day on, his abuse turned to neglect punctuated only by his usual insults.

So yeah, Eddie was right; maybe Billy was trying to be the hero now. He knew he couldn't do anything as dramatic as what Joe had, but ever since that night, he'd been trying to make good on the debt, little by little, so that the cumulative effect might make him feel better about himself.

What Eddie didn't know, though, what Billy had a hard time admitting to himself, was that there were times when he wished Joe hadn't been home that night.

Silenced, Billy turned his attention back to the pastry box and read that one serving contained 365 calories, 17 grams of fat and no dietary fiber. He finally looked up again at Eddie, the only person he had ever entrusted with an account of that evening.

"I hate it when you freakin' nail me," Billy said.

"Yeah, I know you do. And I love it when ya take my advice. Y'oughtta do it more often—like now," Eddie replied. "Make the call, Billy, and I'll make our little visionary here a bologna sandwich."

Billy retreated to the closet out back that Eddie called his office, and Eddie stepped into the cooler to get a new log of bologna. While they were gone, someone passing by the window caught Robby's eye—she had a familiar face, a very familiar face. He jumped off the cooler and trotted to the glass door. Now he could see her only from behind as she walked down the street with a man, but he recognized the coat she was wearing and the way she tilted her head. It was the lady who sat and rocked with him every afternoon, but not today. No, today they didn't rock together. A swell of desire, wordless but strong, moved him to slip out the door and run until he had caught up with her.

14 - The Dorchester Express

A few minutes after Edna had slipped into the Suburban and nodded off, Rita Costello glided out of her house, wearing a smile almost bright enough to melt the light coating of snow on her windshield. In one hand, she carried a pink canvas bag with her initials monogrammed in lime green. It was brimming with design magazines, fabric swatches, and wallpaper samples; and in the other hand, fresh-baked cinnamon rolls, wrapped in homespun and nestled in a wicker basket. After depositing her goods in the rear cargo bed, she got behind the wheel and still smiling, shook her head in a wise, motherly way.

"I *knew* she'd call," she practically sang. "I knew it all along."

"She" was Rita's youngest daughter, Bridget, who had finally—*finally!*—called her mother to ask for help decorating her apartment. To be honest, Rita would have admitted that she had *not* known all along that this call would come, that she had despaired of Bridget's ever doing anything normal again after she'd dropped out of the art history program at

Vassar last year and transferred to the Berklee School to major in music therapy.

"Music therapy! What's that?" a distraught Rita had asked her husband, Charlie. "Singing to crazy people?"

After graduation, when Bridget took a studio apartment in a renovated organ factory in

Dorchester—well, Rita thought the girl was lost for good. Imagine going back to the same declining neighborhood that Charlie had worked so hard to lift them out of fifteen years ago! And living in an old building across the street from a subway station! In one big room that had no wall-to-wall! With a graffiti artist whose name sounded like a disease—Pollux. Somebody ought to be singing to *her*.

Since yesterday's call, though, Rita had been floating, buoyed by the hope that her wayward little lamb was returning to the fold.

"It may be just a first step," Rita had said to Charlie that morning, "but maybe the next one will be finishing her degree in art history, and the one after that will be getting a good job at a museum and then a decent apartment overlooking the Charles River or Boston Harbor and not the Red Line tracks."

"Yeah," Charlie had replied, with a killjoy tone in his voice, "or maybe she just likes where she is and wants some rugs and curtains?"

Rita refused to let his nightmare scenario squelch her spirits, which were still soaring as she backed out of the driveway and headed into the city.

Forty minutes later, though, her mood darkened as she circled the blocks near Bridget's building in search of a space that required neither parallel parking, which she hadn't done since moving to the suburbs, nor too long a walk on streets that looked even grimier than she remembered. One moment, Rita grimaced at volcanoes of trash spewing from uncovered barrels and ripped plastic bags; the next, she subvocalized a "Hail Mary" as a panhandler with a twisted grin, a menacing stare, and a cardboard sign stating the obvious—DOWN AND OUT—approached the car. Through divine intercession, or so she believed, the traffic light she had been stuck at turned green just in time to rescue her from his advance.

As she rounded the corner onto Dorchester Avenue, a dairy truck pulled away from the curb, presenting a spacious spot, but Rita groaned when she saw its proximity to Eddie Jack's, that seedy old grocery Bridget raved about for its "authenticity" and "character." When Rita let herself be dragged inside on the day of Bridget's housewarming party ("*House?*" Rita said to Charlie later. "It's more like a . . . a . . . *cavern!*"), she was not surprised that the store was as much of a no-class dump as it always had been. She found the same dingy, cracked linoleum, narrow aisles cluttered with empty carts and unpacked cartons of Hamburger Helper and Pop Tarts, and the now-old man wearing his signature battered fedora and a bloody apron, but—surprise, surprise—no porcini mushrooms, artisan bread or fresh pesto. Wondering for the umpteenth time how Bridget's sensibilities had become so skewed, Rita took the parking space and got out of the car. She was about to retrieve her bag and basket when she saw the panhandler coming toward her—but no, it was a different one, older and even shadier, an ill-shaven stumblebum in filthy work clothes. As he got closer, he licked his lips and shot her a lecherous gaze, at which Rita's eyebrows popped up like bread out of a toaster. With a horrified cry, she slammed the rear door shut and clutching her purse to her heaving chest, dashed down the street.

♦ ♦ ♦

The noise awakened Edna, who sat up and sniffed.

"Oooh, it smells like somebody made cinnamon rolls," she said in a sing-song voice and followed the scent to the cargo bed.

"They must have left them on the bus. Well, finders, keepers; losers, weepers."

She plucked a roll from the basket, took a bite, and closed her eyes.

"Mmmmm, these are scrumptious! Mutti and Rosamund will love them!"

As she continued munching, the memory of an old, familiar habit occurred to her.

"Jeesh! I almost forgot to pay my fare."

A search of her pockets produced no money, so she settled on her silver identification bracelet.

"This will do quite nicely," she said, as she slipped it off her wrist and then put it into a cup holder.

With the basket on her arm, she scooched out of the van and had just started to walk up the street when she noticed the same man Rita had fled from a few minutes earlier. Edna saw him differently, though. To her eyes, he looked sad and lost, very lost.

"Excuse me, sir," she said brightly, "but would you like a . . . a . . . one of these?"

She handed him a roll and with it, a smile like a day in June.

"Yeah, well . . . sure," he said and then took a bite. "Whoa, these are good. Thanks, lady."

As he chewed, he looked at her, his heavy eyebrows held low.

"You look wicked familiar," he said. "I'm not kiddin', just like somebody I used to know."

"How nice."

"Wait a minute!"

He stepped over to the window of Eddie Jack's store and scanned the black-and-white photos on display.

Pointing at one of Eddie, with a full head of hair and no hat, at the checkout counter next to a girl with bedroom eyes and a killer smile, he beckoned Edna to the window and said, "This is you, ain't it? You used to work here."

"Well, if you say so."

"You're Edna, right? Edna McDonough. Used to be Edna Hogan?"

"Why, that sounds *very* familiar! I believe you're right."

"A'course I'm right. A face like yours you don't forget, darlin'. It always did me in—and so

did the rest of ya."

"Well, I hope you didn't mind."

"Mind? No way! You were a hot tomato, Edna. Hey, don't tell me you've forgotten doin' it with ol' Leo Nee in the back of the delivery truck."

"Okay, I won't, but . . . what were we doing?"

"Well, gettin' it on, a'course. What did you used to call it? *Physical activity*, that was it!"

"Ohhhh. I was good at that."

"Good? Honey, you rocked it!"

"You mean, I was a wild ride?"

"And then some. You were my first lay—um, lady—Edna, and my best ever. Ya spoiled me!"

"Oh, I'm so sorry."

"Don't be, don't be. Wouldn'ta missed it for nothin', especially the night we scored a hat trick in my old man's Rambler, and then there was the time we. . . . Say, you wanna go grab a drink for old time's sake? It's on me—well, on my kid, actually. He don't know it, but he floated me a loan this morning."

"Well, I do need to pop into the market to get some gray corn beef for supper. It's Sweety's favorite, you know. I am kind of thirsty, though."

"Sweety? But he's. . . . Ohhh, I get it. Honey, you do need a drink. Come on."

15 - Skeletons, Hiccups, and Celery

Maggie crossed the yard back to the house and entered through the basement to get onions for the soup. Her desire to make it had faded, but she was determined to finish it anyway as a show of faith in Sweety's providence. He was the one, after all, who had taught her that it wasn't enough to just say you believed in something; you had to act on it.

"If you don't, Mags," Sweety had told her, "then maybe it's just dime store faith, y'know—a cheap imitation."

All Maggie wanted to do right now was to sit in Edna's chair by the window and rock, but she needed to show Sweety that she really believed he would watch over Edna and somehow get her home tonight, probably cold and hungry, but unharmed. And didn't Edna always say that there's nothing like cream of potato soup when you're cold and hungry?

Maggie walked to the wooden crate where her garden onions were stored. There weren't many left, but she managed to find a few firm ones. As she turned toward the stairs, she saw Wil's bicycle helmet hanging from a peg and below it, his white racing bike on its wall-mounted rack. At the sight of them, she gasped, as if a skeleton had just jumped out at her and shouted, "*You haven't called Wil! You're having a crisis, and you haven't called Wil!*"

"Oh, God . . . how could I . . ." she whispered, staring at the wall as if addressing the apparition.

The skeleton produced a succession of endings for this thought, which resounded in her head: "*Forget him? Leave him out? Get along fine without him?*"

Each suggestion made Maggie unsteady, sort of the way she had felt as a seven-year-old when she finally let go of Sweety's hand as they skated at the metropolitan rink in South Boston, and she wobbled along the ice on her own with scores of taller, more agile people speeding by her. Except now there was no rush of excitement to counter the swirling disorientation and rising unease.

"*Why? Don't you need him anymore?*" the skeleton continued in a cool, provocative tone.

Maggie continued toward the stairs, eager to dismiss the question, to take her onions upstairs and make her soup—rather, call Wil and then make her soup. But the urgency of defending herself stopped her.

"I've been, like, in shock, all mixed up, worried sick about Edna. Okay, I forgot to call Wil, but it's not like I don't need him. That's ridiculous. I always needed Wil. I mean, I always *do.* He gives me direction, like my mother used to, and that . . . relieves the stress of being so . . . I don't know—indecisive."

"*It certainly seems like you're calling the shots pretty well today,*" the skeleton observed.

"Maybe, but I'm a still a wreck. That's probably why I forgot to call him. If I had, I would have been calmer because he would have been sure of what to do, and I mean, anybody that sure has to be right, don't they?"

"*What about the time he wanted to send Robby away?*" the skeleton countered.

"Well, okay, sure, but . . . but you can't expect him to have the instincts of a mother. That wouldn't be fair. Besides, other than that . . ."

"*There was the time he wanted to put Edna into an old-age home.*"

"That's unfair, too. So, he doesn't have the instincts of a daughter either—how could he?

Anyway, those were just . . . exceptions. Look, he was the one who was sure we should get married, that we were meant for each other. I didn't disagree. I just wasn't as sure as he was, but I was never sure about anything, so I trusted him. And he turned out to be right, didn't he? Here we are, ten years later, still together."

In response, the skeleton switched from audio to video, and suddenly Maggie saw herself walking down the aisle of Saint Aloysius Church looking like a large dollop of meringue—white and poofy and kind of stiff—in a wedding gown Mrs. Dodge had assured her was elegant. Her uncle Arthur handed her over to Wil at the altar. As always, he looked poised, relaxed, certain.

Father Keegan began chanting prayers. Maggie's eyes wandered nervously—she really hated being the center of attention—and finally settled on a framed portrait of Jesus Christ, his exposed heart glowing and encircled with thorns. The image, familiar and usually unremarkable, prompted her to recall an unresolved Sweety Dream she had had a few days earlier.

In this one, she and a throng of other young women in wedding gowns were in the produce section of a market, where an entire display case was filled with small bags of celery. Her companions were examining each of them with scrupulous care before making their choices, but Maggie simply stood by, watching them until Diego Ortega, in a greengrocer's apron, handed her a bag.

"NO, NO, NO!" the other women shouted in chorus. "MAGGIE'S GOT TO LOOK AROUND! SHE'S GOT TO MAKE HER OWN *CHOICE*!"

At this, Ortega shook his head, and the dream faded.

The pressure of Wil's hand on hers brought her back to the ceremony, specifically to the vows Father Keegan was asking her to repeat. And as she began, so did the hiccups.

"I, Marg-hic-aret, do take thee Wil-hic-ford . . ."

With the second line, their pace and volume picked up so that the church echoed with what

sounded like an offshoot of Pig Latin.

"To-hic-be-hic-my-hic-law-hic-ful-hic-hus-hic . . ."

At this point, an altar boy was dispatched to the sacristy for a glass of water. By the time he returned, Edna and her aunts Gert and Rosamund were at Maggie's side, offering conflicting prescriptions.

"Drink it backwards, honey," Edna advised.

Gert scoffed.

"Backwards? That never works. Sip it between deep breaths."

"Listen to the two of you," Rosamund declared. "Just chug it and say a silent Hail Mary."

After all three methods had failed, Father Keegan proceeded to read the vows as one long question. When he got to the end, ". . . until death do you part," a Vesuvian hiccup jolted Maggie's head in an upward-downward motion that he took as an assent. Wil then breezed through his part of the script and kissed her, ending the bizarre spasm of her glottis.

Moments later, though, as Maggie and Wil were posing for the photographer at the door of the church, the key to the Sweety Dream—or so she thought—revealed itself to her: the *heart* of celery comes in small plastic bags. The heart! The symbol of love! With the bridal chorus's words echoing in her head ("Maggie's got to make her *own* choice!"), Maggie looked at Wil with a tight, borderline panicky expression atypical of a wife of less than five minutes.

I didn't do it the right way! *I didn't look around*! *I didn't make my own choice*! *But how could I*? *I suck at decision making*!

In sprinting to these conclusions, Maggie failed to consider the significance of Ortega, Sweety's old alter ego, who, as usual, required thoughtful interpretation.

When Wil noticed Maggie's unbride-like expression, a quizzical frown clouded his face, but he soon transformed it into a smile, as if she were smiling at him. So, she did smile, and her sudden doubt—no, she couldn't call it anything as serious as *doubt*. *Qualm*, maybe, *fleeting qualm*—disappeared like the hiccups with no further thought of celery.

"*You used to like celery*," the bike-skeleton in the basement now told her, "*but you've lost your taste for it, haven't you? You never use it in soup anymore. Hmmm . . . interesting.*"

"But . . . but that doesn't mean . . ."

Maggie was spared further inquisition by the sound of a phone ringing. Reflexively, she reached into her back pocket and on finding it empty, sprinted up the stairs to the kitchen.

She saw her new iPhone glowing on the table, where she had left it when she ran out to the shed, but by the time she reached it, it was silent. Against Robby's placid image, though, a notification appeared.

WIL: Two Missed Calls.

As Maggie's finger was poised over his number, the phone rang again.

16 - Not So Sure

"I appreciate your curiosity about Holy Orders, Eamon," Monsignor Canny said, and then paused for a sip of Guinness. "But it might be premature to get into the particulars of that right now."

He pivoted his head, shot Wil a snide grin, and said, "Unless *you'd* like to, Wil. I hear from Eamon that you have quite an interest in our Catholic liturgy."

Wil set down his glass of scotch and shot right back.

"Oh, wouldn't I just love to, Father, but I don't want to slow things down."

"Ah, how good of you." Turning again to the pitcher, the monsignor said, "What you need to consider first, Eamon, is that becoming a priest is a lot like getting married. It's about love and devotion, of course, but sacrifice, too—a joyful willingness to put aside purely selfish desires and consider instead the needs of others."

Eamon nodded. Wil frowned.

"Another thing to think about is that the priesthood, like marriage, is not something to be chosen merely because it suits a set of preferences or feeds the ego. In fact, neither one should be a choice at all because each, in its own way, is a calling. Like love for another person, the priesthood is a . . . treasure God has placed inside you. Finding it may not always be easy, and in fact, it is often quite hard, as I believe you've discovered. But once you do find it, you have no choice but to embrace it because it's what God meant for you. You might say it's the God within you."

Upon hearing the priest's last words Eamon's eyebrows, his color, the corners of his mouth rose in glorious unison. If this had been a movie, rays of sunlight would have streamed through the window, and the old men at the bar would have turned toward him and broken into a chorus of "Alleluia." The pitcher's reaction should have troubled Wil, but it didn't because he had stopped paying attention to Eamon as the priest presented his conception of marriage. It struck a nerve Wil didn't know he had, like the one that had been making his eyelid flutter intermittently since Eamon went missing. This one was even more annoying, and to quell it, he mounted a retort.

How do you goddamn celibates come up with this crap? Joyful sacrifice? Gimme a break! What the hell do you know about marriage? All you do is wear robes, chant prayers, and pound down Jack Daniels at the reception. As if that doesn't feed your ego and suit your preferences. And by the way, ego is what wannabes call self-confidence, and preferences are like . . . priorities. Losers don't have them. Winners do.

Wil didn't give voice to his rant, though. Instead, he heard himself say, "Excuse me, "I've . . . uh . . . got to make a call."

Monsignor Canny replied, "Nothing wrong, I hope."

"No, no, no. It's just . . . something I forgot."

He retreated to a nearby booth and pulled out his phone. Looking up for a moment, he saw a skinny, young waitress, her eyes riveted on the trembling tray she was carrying, bump into the monsignor's chair and lose control of her cargo. Reflexively, Eamon, one of the best-fielding pitchers in the league the previous year, reached out with both hands and made the grab. The woman dropped into Wil's vacated chair, gasping, a hand splayed on her chest, and squealed, "Ohmygod! Ohmygod!" until she noticed the monsignor's collar and apologized for taking the Lord's name in vain.

"In this case," the priest replied, "I really don't think He minds."

She was halfway to her feet when she recognized Eamon. Her eyes bulged, as if the pope himself were before her holding a bottle of beer. Again, she dropped into the chair.

"Ohmygod! You're . . . you're . . . lost or something."

Eamon took a swig and looked at Monsignor Canny with a serene smile.

"I was," he said, "but not anymore."

As Wil observed the scene, his memory called up another little drama with a different bumbling waitress.

Then a college junior, Wil was eating chicken gumbo and reading a book for his Irish history class at the Soupremes Café, a retro diner in Amherst. He noticed the waitress, not because she was particularly hot—she wasn't—but because when she stepped out of the kitchen carrying a tray with a bowl of soup, a salad, and a pint glass of iced coffee, she looked panicky, as if she had just been pushed onstage in the middle of a play she hadn't even read. He watched as she crept toward a nearby table, hardly glancing up from the tray, and was surprised when she managed to get there without incident. He winced, though, as she attempted to hold the tray with one hand and transfer the salad with the other. As he'd expected, the tray tipped, sending the bowl and the glass crashing to the floor. The customer, a junior-prof type in chinos, a turtleneck, and a tweed sports jacket jumped up and surveyed his pant legs, which had only a few splotches on them.

"Shit!" he screeched. "You goddamn idiot! I'll . . ."

Wil was out of his seat and in the guy's face.

"Here, you fuckin' wuss," he said, slamming a ten-dollar bill onto the table. "Get your Dockers dry-cleaned, and while you're at it, see if they do mouths, too."

Wil hoped the jerk would throw a punch, so he'd have an excuse to flatten him, but before either of them could commit to the next move, a woman intervened. It was as if Gladys Knight had descended from the galaxy of Motown stars whose photos were framed on the walls. She grabbed the prof's arm and fired him a look that made the guy gulp.

"You go home to your mama and learn some manners before you come back to my establishment, fool," she bellowed as she muscled him out the door.

Then she stalked back to the table where Wil was still standing, picked up his money, and thrust it into his shirt pocket.

"You ever see trouble in here again, Sir Galahad," she said, with a finger poke to his chest, "you keep your butt parked and let Erylene handle it. Now go eat your soup."

Turning to the waitress, whose face had flushed to sunburn pink, she said, "Maggie, do better, girl. Lots better."

Later, when Maggie brought Wil his check and thanked him, he told her that the only thanks he would accept was a date. He wasn't sure what it was, but something about her appealed to him. A few nights later, over dinner at Shanghai Gardens, he found out.

"I suck at waitressing," she told him. "I really, really do, but I need the money for school, so I guess in a way I'm lucky, but what I'd really like to do is work in the kitchen because I'm pretty good at making soup—I learned it from my mother—but I don't want to seem pushy and ask for special treatment, because Erylene's my roommate's aunt, and she's already been so nice to me even when I drop trays and screw up orders and . . . well, everything, but still I'm really kind of miserable and, well . . . what do you think I should do, Wil?"

The outpouring of confusion, self-doubt, and neediness on a first date might have turned other guys off, but Wil was charmed, and like a ref, ready with his call: "She likes you. Ask her. You can't lose."

When they met for coffee the following week, he discovered something else appealing about her.

"So I did what you said, and it worked—it *really* worked, so now I'm in the kitchen and I make $1.50 more an hour, and best of all, Erylene loved my butternut squash soup, especially when I told her that the secret ingredient was apple butter, her favorite—who knew?—and she even told me it was 'Soupreme soup' and oh, Wil, thank you so much because I wouldn't have had the nerve to do it without you."

Wil had never really helped anyone enough to receive this much gratitude, and he found that he liked it, was hungry for more, in fact, which he couldn't say about the butternut squash soup she had brought him in a plastic container.

Over time, he also learned that Maggie's dilemma wasn't that she didn't have her own opinions; on the contrary, her mind housed a teeming brood of them that argued over everything: what courses to take, what major to declare, what color to paint her bedroom. Instead of arbitrating, though, she sympathized with all of them to the point of paralysis. Wil, whose father had taught him that he would never win at anything if he didn't trust his hunches and his ability to assess odds, loved it when Maggie called him in to get her moving. She wasn't anywhere near as good looking as the other girls he had dated, but the way she craved his opinions—ate them up, really—was a surprisingly satisfying substitute. He could never go wrong, either, because he would satisfy Maggie not just by giving her advice that ultimately succeeded, but by giving her any advice at all.

And, Wil now recalled, it had been that way ever since. Well, there was that weird moment after their wedding ceremony when they were standing arm in arm in the doorway of Saint Aloysius Church, about to step outside. Maggie turned and looked at him as if . . . well, now that Wil thought back on it, as if she'd just been pushed onstage in the middle of a play she hadn't even read. Confused. Lost, even. For a frightening moment, she looked as if she were going to tell him that she had changed her mind. But he knew that she hadn't made up her mind in the first place. He had: "We were meant for each other, Mags," he had told her by way of proposal. "I know it. I *feel* it. We're a win-win, for sure."

So, as she seemed to waver on the threshold of their life together, he produced his most confident, reassuring smile, and after a few seconds, she smiled back. Win-win never failed.

Except maybe for that . . . aberration when Maggie stood up to him about Robby's schooling. At the time, Wil was sure that she was just overwrought and that sooner or later, with more reasoning and maybe a little coaxing, he would get her to come around to his way of thinking. When she held firm, as if she had been inoculated against his persuasiveness, he flashed back to that look she'd given him in the church doorway. It was the first time in years he had thought about it, and he found himself worrying: Had he lost his ability to influence her? Was she going to start questioning him about other things, too? Could the balance that had always worked for them disintegrate?

But none of that happened.

Although there was that one other time when they knew Edna couldn't live on her own anymore, and he pushed to send her to a continuing care nursing home—not some dumping ground, either, but a high-end one in Wellesley Hills with gardens and a therapeutic swimming pool and a bona fide chef—and Maggie pushed right back, insisting that Edna come to live with them. Again, he recalled the doorway look; again, he worried.

That turned out to be just another aberration, though. Things got right back to normal, and they've stayed that way. Just a couple of weeks ago, Maggie couldn't decide whether to switch to an iPhone or keep her android, and when he told her to stick with what she was used to, she said, "Yeah, I guess that makes sense." He couldn't remember now what kind of phone she eventually bought, but he was sure it must be another android.

The thought of her cell phone reminded him of his reason for being there in the booth: to get in touch with Maggie, to make sure there was no problem at home. The priest's drivel about marriage—well, that was kind of a harsh way to describe it—got him thinking about her again: Why didn't she pick up either phone when he called earlier? And if she was busy then, why didn't she call him back later? She always called him back. What if something *was* wrong?

Maybe Edna had a stroke, or maybe the school van had an accident and Robby was hurt. But that didn't make sense because then Maggie would definitely have called—definitely. She'd never handle something like that by herself. She'd need Wil to lean on, to make decisions. She'd always needed him—well, except for the occasional aberration. So, why didn't she answer? And why was he seeing her face in the church doorway again?

Wil's phone rang. He swiped the screen without a glance and pressed the phone to his ear.

"Maggie?" he said, with urgency that startled him.

"No such luck, Dodgeball." Pop! "Make me happy."

"I . . . can't do that, Richie," he said.

"YOU GOTTA BE FUCKIN' KIDDIN' M . . ."

Wil cut him off and called Maggie. After getting voicemail again both on her cell and the land line, he rushed back to the table.

Eamon was still glowing. Not even after pitching that no-hitter against the Yankees in New York did Wil ever see him glow.

"Part of me feels really dumb for taking so long to know my own heart," the pitcher was telling the priest. "It's just that most everybody else was so sure about what was right for me. I just trusted them."

He took a deep breath, as if the beery atmosphere of the Connemara were a fresh ocean breeze.

"But the other part of me? Well, like you said, monsignor, it feels like I found a treasure, and I'm finally ready to trust myself."

When Monsignor Canny saw Wil, he said, "So, Wil, it looks like the good Lord might have a prospect here. I know you might not . . ."

"Yeah, well, great," Wil said. All he wanted was to get away from all this joyful holiness and self-discovery, go home, find his wife there, and get back to win-win, preferably with no more aberrations. When he saw Eamon's crestfallen expression, though, he was embarrassed by his curtness.

"I mean, it *is* great. Really. You look . . . happy, kiddo. And I guess you have to go with it. No choice, right, padre?"

Wil noticed Monsignor Canny looking at him, like that painting of Saint Francis had earlier. This time, the penetrating gaze didn't put him off, though. It made him want to sit down and tell the priest what was really on his mind and to hear the holy man offer reassurances in a comforting tone that would get that doorway look on Maggie's face out of his head. What was he going to say, though? That he suddenly felt unsure about . . . what? His wife's dependence on him? Win-win? His preferences and ego? He couldn't. It was too . . . crazy. Instead, he made a lame-sounding excuse about another appointment, said goodbye, and headed toward the door.

"Wil," Monsignor Canny called after him. "I hope you find what you're looking for, too."

17 - An Unlikely Saint

Rita Costello couldn't find her car. Earlier, she couldn't find her daughter, who apparently forgot that she had invited her mother for a visit today and was not home at the appointed time, leaving Rita to wait on the sidewalk with a dead cell phone, as she tried both to avoid eye contact with and to keep a defensive eye on wave after wave of intimidating characters who emerged from the subway station across the street. There were silent, slouchy boys in voluminous pants and hooded jackets that concealed God-knows-what weapons; loud, scurrilous girls squeezed into denim pants as tight as their expressions; forlorn men and women who looked too tired to walk, but not too tired to mug a fashionably dressed and utterly defenseless suburbanite. It was a reality horror show!

After forty minutes, Rita's endurance ran out, and she launched a frantic hunt for her car, which so far had produced nothing except regret that she'd let her membership at the Chestnut Hill Fitness Club lapse five years ago and that she listened to Charlie whenever he told her that they shouldn't meddle in Bridget's life. So now she was fat and out of shape, and her daughter was not going to be a doctoral candidate in art history at Harvard or BU, but an inner-city bohemian who taught nutcases to play the lute but ignored her own mother. And as if all that wasn't bad enough, Rita was gripped by the steadily rising apprehension that she was going to be wandering these grimy streets *forever.*

Suddenly her chest tightened, and heat exploded on her face as her heart started to pummel her chest from inside. She had watched enough episodes of *ER* and *Grey's Anatomy* to know what was happening. She was having a heart attack! With this thought, her symptoms not only worsened, but also multiplied: her breathing was labored, her mouth was dry, her arms were numb. She was going to die! On Dot Ave! The horror of this inevitability pushed her to stagger on in her search of the Suburban, where she could plug her phone in and call for help, or at least pass away in comfort and privacy.

Then she remembered the panic button on her key thingy. It had helped her countless times at shopping malls, where you practically had to be a genius to remember where you parked. It could help her now! It was right in her pocket! But after she pressed it, she heard nothing but the steady drone of traffic and a few far-off sirens.

Out of options, out of energy, out of luck, Rita was ready to collapse onto the cold, wet pavement when she saw a ray of light in the late afternoon gloom.

"Wil Dodge? Wil Dodge!" she cried out with all the volume she could muster.

♦ ♦ ♦

Wil was half-jogging back to his car when he heard a shrill voice call his name. Up ahead, he saw an overweight, unnaturally blonde, and apparently drunk woman in a lavender pants suit waving a pink scarf and staggering toward him.

"Mrs. Costello?" he asked as she drew closer.

"I'm . . . saved! I'm . . . saved!" was her only reply.

"Mrs. Costello, what . . . what are you doing here?"

Rita mopped her brow with the scarf.

"Dying! That's . . . what I'm doing . . . *was* doing. Now I'm . . . saved."

"Dying? Saved? Mrs. Costello, have you been drinking?"

"I . . . wish. I've been. . . . Oh! Oh!"

Gasping, she clutched his arm.

Now alarmed, Wil said, "Mrs. Costello, I'm going to call an ambulance."

He stuck his hand into his empty pocket, patted himself down, and muttered, "Shit!"

"That's . . . what I say," Rita sputtered.

At this moment, a tall, wiry man in paint-stained overalls emerged from a nearby building and was hurrying toward his pick-up truck when he noticed Wil and Rita's distress.

"You guys need help?" he called over to them.

"Yes!" Wil and Rita cried in unison.

"She's got to get to a hospital fast. Can you call 9-1-1 for her?" Wil asked.

"I can do better," the man replied as he approached them. "I'm just now goin' back to pick up my crew at a job they're finishin' right near Boston Hospital. I know a quick route, too. I can have ya to the ER before an ambulance could even get here. We can call ahead and let them know we're on our way."

"No, no, no," was Wil's knee-jerk response.

"Hell, YES!" was Rita's.

Wil grimaced as he uttered his least favorite sentence: "I . . . I don't know."

"Buddy, it looks like the clock's tickin' here."

Rita commanded Wil in a grisly tone. "Get me . . . out of . . . here!"

"Okay! Okay! Take her," he told the painter.

They led Rita to the truck, and Wil watched as the painter settled her into the back seat of the cab, putting his jacket around her shoulders and buckling the safety belt. He was so gentle with her, so solicitous. He was putting himself out for her, too, and she was a total stranger to him.

"What's your name, ma'am?" he asked.

"Rita. And you're . . . ?"

"Francis," he replied, a serene smile blossoming above his dark brown goatee. "My name's

Francis."

As Francis took the wheel, Rita looked up at Wil, who was still looking in from the sidewalk, and she said, "You're coming with me, aren't you, Wil?"

"Oh, I can't . . ." Wil began.

What he was about to say was suddenly erased, as if someone had pressed a delete button in his brain and recorded the words that did come out of his mouth, serenely, in his own voice. And Wil knew just who that someone was.

"Can't very well let you go alone, can I?" he heard himself say against instinct and logic. "I'm . . . glad to help."

After he had climbed in next to her, she took hold of his hand. Her eyes were overflowing.

"You're a saint, Wil Dodge. A saint."

18 - Confession

Edna and Robby were nestled in the same booth that Wil had left so hurriedly just a few minutes earlier. Her eyes were focused on Leo as he approached the table carrying two drinks. When he set one of them, an Old Fashioned, in front of her, her smile burst forth, radiating childlike delight.

"Oh, a . . . a . . . little brown glass!" she exclaimed.

"See?" Leo replied. "I even remembered what you drink."

He put the other glass in front of Robby and said, "I hope ya like ginger ale, kiddo."

As if in reply, Robby picked up the glass and took a big gulp.

"Hey, he's got a stroke like yours, Edna."

Leo returned to the bar and came back with a bottle of beer and a bag of pretzels, which he ripped open and placed in the middle of the table.

"Just a few hors d'oeuvres. Ha!"

He settled in across from her, but just as he started to drink, he noticed something on the far side of the bench.

"Well, well, well," he chimed as he reached over and snapped up a cell phone. "Look what somebody left behind. How'd they know I've always wanted one of these?"

"Maybe it's your birthday?" Edna replied brightly.

"It is now," he said, pocketing the phone. "Cheers, Edna. Cheers. What did you say his name is?"

"He's Robby."

"Cheers, Robby."

As Leo took a swig, Edna looked around, slightly squinting.

"You know, I think maybe I was here once."

"Once? Honey, I heard they kept a stool reserved for ya."

"That was very kind of them."

"Me? I got to be a Bantry Bay guy until me and the owner got into a financial dispute, due to him bein' a cheap asshole—pardon my French—who won't let a loyal customer such as myself run a reasonable tab."

"Asshole," Edna repeated softly. "Yes, it does sound better in French. Don't you think so, Robby?"

Robby, munching pretzels, looked at her and smiled.

"He don't say much, does he?" Leo observed.

"Why, he doesn't have to," Edna replied as she planted a kiss on Robby's head.

"Well, it don't bother me none. I'm at the age where I like it quiet. That's why I sometimes come in here this time of day. Later on, ya gotta listen to the goddamn yuppies when they pile in here after work. But now it's just right for us to, y'know, catch up."

Edna sipped her drink and nodded, the once-familiar warmth of Jim Beam coloring her cheeks almost immediately.

Muffled music emanated from Leo's pants. He pulled the phone out of his pocket and saw a

green circle with the words *Press to Accept* in white letters below it. Curious, he touched it and

heard a woman's distant voice. He couldn't find the mouthpiece, so he put his lips up to the screen.

"I can't talk," he growled. Then he added something he had always wanted to say, something he'd heard just about every time he asked some asshole for a job: "And don't call us. We'll call you."

He stuffed the phone back into his pocket and took another swig of beer.

"Sorry. Where was I? Oh, yeah, catchin' up. You know, Edna, as soon as I recognized you today, the memories all came back to me—y'know, all the good times and how hard I fell for ya. What was it, fifty years ago? Jeez. And I'm not just talkin' about the physical activity, neither."

Edna sipped, flushed, nodded. Robby watched her and sipped, too.

"I was only seventeen, but I was so sure we woulda made an awesome couple. I mean, we both loved to cut loose and never the hell mind what anybody else thought. You remember that night we got hammered over at L Street Beach and went skinny dippin'—in November? It started snowin' for Chrissake, but we didn't care. We were havin' a blast! And that's what I thought life could be like if we stayed together, a never-endin' blast. Hmph. Remember what you said when I told you that?"

When he saw Edna's sweet, vacuous smile, his rough, weary features softened.

"No. A'course ya don't. Well, let me remind ya: 'Parties can't last forever, Leo. You have to dance with as many partners as you can.' So, a while later, you moved on to the next one, and I did, too. Had a lot of fun. Then along came Betty—Betty Cronin."

"Betty," Edna repeated, her eyes alight with recognition. "Ohhh, Betty was a *good* girl."

"That she was. The parish saint, right? And obviously way too good for yours truly. But the

weird thing was, she didn't think so. She was sure I had somethin' good in me, too. Said she could just feel it. Well, at first I thought it was a lot of bullshit—pardon my . . ."

"French?" Edna interjected.

"Yeah, honey. French. Except Betty wasn't the bullshittin' type. And y'know, it made me *feel* good that someone like her thought I was more than a tough-ass punk. Not that I wasn't kinda proud of my rep—drinkin', fightin', skippin' work, y'know, everything my parole officer told me not to do. But I didn't want to do that to Betty, so for a while, I cleaned up my act—held down a job, went to Sunday mass, even laid off the sauce, for Chrissake. Then, as ya may know, we got married, and, well, pretty soon the tough-ass punk showed up again, and it was like I spent the next twenty years tryin' to prove that Betty'd been wrong after all. Did a damn good job of it, too, especially after the kid came."

"Robby?" Edna asked.

"Uh, no . . . we named him Billy."

"Billy. He must be a good boy."

"Oh, he's got a lot of his mother in him. That's for sure. Too much, maybe. I remember when he was little, he was just so damn eager to please—y'know. 'Can I shovel the sidewalk? Can I set the table? Can I run to the store?' And smart? Cripes, he was always bringin' home papers with gold stars and report cards with all A's, includin' conduct.

"Problem was, everything he did pissed me off. But for a while, anyway, he just kept tryin' to get me to like him, which pissed me off even more. I can't even tell ya why, Edna, 'cause to this day I don't know myself. All I can say is I kinda turned into my old man, may the devil turn up the oven on him. I say 'kinda' because even though I whacked Billy around a lot, I never beat the crap outta him—well, at least when Betty was alive—like the bastard did to me. Christ, he broke my jaw when I was nine years old. *Nine*."

Leo's lips tightened, and his eyes turned toward the TV above the bar, as if he were watching a replay of the Christmas Eve when Leo Sr. stumbled into their apartment from the Bantry Bay and unleashed his longshoreman's fist into his son's face for trying to restrain him from beating up his wife.

"You'da thought I of all people would never do that kind of shit to my own kid—y'know, that I'd spare him all the . . . the pain, I guess. But I didn't. I didn't . . ."

Edna did not understand much of what the man across from her had been saying, but she'd enjoyed listening to the low timbre of his voice. Now, as it trailed off, she wanted him to start talking and looking happy again.

"I think I'd like another little brown glass," she said. "How about you . . . my friend?"

Without waiting for a response, she revived an old reflex by shooting an arm into the air and twirling a finger to signal the bartender for another round.

"That's my girl, Edna," Leo said, with a sad smile. "You know just what I need."

After he returned with the drinks, he shifted the spotlight onto her.

"Long story short, I sucked at turnin' over a new leaf, but you, you did a 180 and never looked back: ladies' sodality, Bible group, Christian doctrine teacher. Before ya married Sweety, rumor was you were goin' into the goddamn convent! I always thought maybe the accident had somethin' to do with all that. I mean, when you survive a car wreck like you were in, I guess it changes ya. Maybe that's what I needed, Edna, a car wreck. But with my luck, I woulda ended up like Jack O'Toole, which, now that I think of it, might have been better for everybody."

The glow of listening and drinking whiskey disappeared from Edna's face.

"Jack O'Toole," she repeated. "I . . . I was in a car with Jack O'Toole."

Leo reached across the table and took her hand.

"It musta been hell, Edna. You're lucky to be alive."

Edna had no clear memory of the night she and Jack O'Toole were speeding home from the Beachfront Club in Wollaston, their heads swimming and their eyes bleary from hours of tequila shots. She couldn't see herself reaching over and unzipping Jack's pants as he drove or sticking her hand inside and rubbing a fleshy mass until it emerged from the fly or bending over and sucking the now-hard protuberance as if it were a big lollipop, nor could she hear Jack's pleasure-filled groans as he closed his eyes and released warm, viscous liquid into her mouth.

Vague, too, were the sounds of the accelerating engine and the explosive crash of the car into a street pole and of the shattering of the windshield as Jack's head was propelled against it.

A part of her brain, though, had stored, and now retrieved the shock she felt when she awoke in the Kearney Hospital the next day and her grim-faced father told her that Jack was in surgery.

"The drunken bastard has all but killed himself, and he might have killed you, too. I warned you he was bad company, Edna. And ask yourself, what kind of girls insist on keepin' bad company?"

Bad. Bad. Bad.

As the guilt and shame that flooded her that day resurged now, so did the memory of kneeling in a confessional box several weeks later, waiting to reveal her sin to a priest—not at Saint A's, but across town at Saint Gabriel's in Brighton where there was no chance her confessor would recognize her voice. Her heartbeat once again quickened as she envisioned the confessional chamber, so dark that she had felt blind, where she'd knelt, waiting in agony until the wooden shutter slid open and revealed the dimly lit profile of a gray-haired priest through a thick screen. Her twenty-four-year-old voice echoed in her head: "Bless me, Father, for I have sinned . . ." and even more clearly, the priest's response after she had finished.

"You have perverted the sanctity of physical union as Our Lord intended it. It is, as you fear, a grievous, grievous sin. As a result, your soul is, at this moment, marked for eternal suffering. But the Almighty and his church forgive those who are sincerely contrite, and I believe you are. To earn that forgiveness, though, you must cast aside the illicit pleasures that have endangered you and solemnly vow to live a worthy life from now until the day you die. A life of purity and love and devotion to others. It is the only thing that can save you. Will you do that? Will you make that vow?"

"Edna. Edna," Leo said softly in an attempt to get her back from wherever she had drifted.

At this moment, though, she spotted a man in black on the other side of the room.

It's the priest. He's here. He's waiting to hear my answer.

Edna pulled her hand away from Leo's, slid out of the booth, and rushed to the table where Monsignor Canny and Eamon Lally were still conversing. She fell to her knees before the priest, clutching his hands and looking up at him like a prisoner begging a judge to spare her life.

"I will, Father! I solemnly vow! I'll be a good girl from now on! Forgive me, Father! Please, *please*, forgive me!"

Leo, who, with Robby in tow, had followed Edna, stood nearby and heard not just her words, but the anguish in her voice. He hadn't unburdened himself before a priest for decades, but he recalled the drill. You weren't supposed to be afraid of God's punishment, but . . . what was the word the nuns used? Contrite. *Sincerely contrite.* Otherwise, you couldn't be truly forgiven, and your soul couldn't be completely cleansed. He wasn't sure what Edna had done, or thought she had done, but for the first time in his life, he got what *sincerely contrite* meant, and her perfect remorse kindled in him a possibility that flickered in his eyes. Maybe for once in his life he could pull it off, too, or come close enough, and then this priest or some other one would declare him cleansed of the ugly, hurtful shit he had done and said over the years. Sure, it was bad—some of it really bad—but maybe it wasn't unforgivable. It could be that bumping into Edna today was a sign or something, telling him that he still had a chance, that he could still be the good guy Betty had thought he was.

At the very thought, though, his accumulated transgressions amassed and surrounded him like rival gang members, pressing closer and closer. The light in his eye went out and his breathing turned heavy as their grip on him tightened until they had suffocated his hope with the force of their malice—his malice, really—and heaved him out the door onto the street.

19 - Good Fortune

"How'd it go with the cops?" Eddie asked when Billy reappeared.

"Well, bottom line, I think I convinced them I'm not guilty of kidnapping, just wicked bad luck."

"And a big, warm stupid heart."

Billy grinned. "Yeah, that, too. Anyway, while I was on hold, they called the principal to get the kid's address, but she doesn't want me to drive him home—something about protocols—so she's going to get in touch with the mother, and then I guess she'll come and get . . ."

Billy's eyes darted left and right. After checking the two small grocery aisles, he said, "Where's the kid, Eddie?"

"I was just going to ask you that. I figured he went back there with you when I was in the cooler."

"You left him alone?"

"For thirty seconds. He seemed so . . . content. I . . . I didn't think . . . he'd leave."

"Yeah, Eddie, except he did! How the hell could you . . ."

Mum in his head, whom Billy hadn't heard in a while, spoke up in her softest, most sympathetic tone.

"Billy, look at him. He feels bad enough. It won't help if you . . ."

Billy held his breath a few seconds and for the first time ever, silently screamed at her through clenched teeth: "*Shut the fuck up and leave me alone, Mum*!" Then he continued his rant.

"Be so goddamn stupid? You were supposed to *help* me, old man, not get me more fucked than I already was. Jesus!"

"Okay, just . . ."

"Just what, Eddie? Just what the fuck am I supposed to do in this situation? Call the cops again? Tell them I lost the kid this time? Or wait until his mother gets here and break the news to her?"

"Let me go find him. He can't have gone far. He's probably in the pizza shop or the bakery, someplace close."

"Oh, sure. And I wait here for mommy. No fuckin' way. *I'll* go look for him."

"Sure, sure. But what do I tell her if she comes before you get back?"

"That's your fuckin' problem, Eddie. I got enough of my own."

♦ ♦ ♦

Billy stepped out of Renzo's Pizza and Subs looking every bit as desperate as he felt. He sank onto an old bench and slouched against the cold wall. His lips were a hard, thin line as he stared into the street with unfocused, hopeless eyes. He had already been to the Avenue Bakery, the Sparkle Laundromat, Tran Huc Produce, Eileen's Flower Shop, and Victory Liquors. Nobody had seen the kid. And mommy was on the way.

His phone rang. He didn't recognize the number on the screen, but his brain was so fried that he answered anyway.

"Billy! It's me, Joe. I got great news, man!"

"Look, Joe, this is a bad time . . ."

The words rang false in his ears because it was actually, a *good* time, a fan*fucking*tastic time, to tell this dumb ass all the crap he'd caused and to wreck whatever good news was making him sound so goddamn infuriatingly happy.

Billy expected Mum in his head to speak up again, to urge him to calm down and be nice, but she didn't. She was doing exactly what he had told her to do. She was leaving him alone. And that's just how he felt now, alone. And shitty about laying into her and shitty about laying into Eddie. Suddenly, he didn't want to feel more alone and shittier by hurting the only other person who had never hurt him, so when Joe prattled on, he listened.

"I sold three of my paintings! And the guy who bought them? He likes them so much, he's going to help me promote the rest of my stuff, kind of like an agent. Unbelievable, right?"

"Yeah, literally," Billy replied.

"And the craziest part of the whole thing is, he knows you!"

Before Billy could utter a word, he heard another voice on the line: "Hey, Billy! Drew Winston again!"

Apparently unfazed by Billy's stunned silence, he continued. "So, okay, Uncle Press and I get up here and the slopes are closed because of icing, so we wander into this art exhibit at the hotel, and I see these paintings that just blow . . . me . . . away."

"Joe's paintings . . . blew you away?"

"Totally. I don't know if I mentioned it to you, but I took some art history at Williams. Anyway, these pieces are like awesome examples of the American neo-primitive genre. They're something so . . . organic and elemental about them. So, I get to talking with Joe, and he mentions that he's from Dorchester, and I play the do-you-know game—and bingo!—I find out you're best buddies."

"Organic and elemental?"

"Right! So, just like that, it all came together. I mean, what I was talking about with you today, finding my passion, and then discovering it in your friend's art. I don't know. It felt like the pieces of some cosmic puzzle had finally come together. Something inside told me to seize the moment. So, I am, Billy. I'm going with it!"

"Seize the moment?"

"Exactly! Anyway, I'll put Joe back on. We'll talk, man."

"Awesome, isn't it, Billy? I told you I was channeling some positive energy today. Wow! But listen, you're in a hurry, so I won't keep you any longer. Oh, but wait . . . how'd the drive go?"

"It was, um, a day I'll never forget." Billy was tempted to add, "No matter how hard I try," but he refrained because he wanted to appease Mum in his head, if she was still there.

"Ha! That makes two of us—well, three. Drew, too. Okay, see ya, pal."

Billy pocketed his phone and lowered his head, as deflated as the crumpled paper bag that scuttled past him in the gutter. His loneliness surged, and as it did, it emptied him of everything except the certainty that he was and would forever be a loser, that the good fortune that shone upon guys like Joe and Drew left him in the dark because, just as Leo always told him, he was worthless. Come to think of it, it was a lot like the feeling he used to have after Leo beat the crap out of him in high school. He had a recurring daydream back then of walking into oncoming traffic. He'd see a truck approaching—it was always a truck, a big one—and he'd hear the squeal of its breaking tires and the thud of his body against the hood. He never imagined any pain, though, just . . . nothing. Sweet, silent nothing. He'd be sitting in class or riding the T home or stocking Eddie's shelves, and suddenly he'd come to, a little shaken and a little disappointed.

Billy stood up at the rumble of a loud vehicle approaching. He looked left up the avenue toward Saint A's and saw a City of Boston garbage truck making the turn from Columbia Road. It was going faster than it should have been, probably heading back to the depot at the end of the workday. He stepped to the edge of the sidewalk and waited, watching the truck get closer and closer, hearing its engine get louder and louder, feeling its vibration permeate him. His teeth and his hands were both clenched.

Still focused on the truck, Billy took a step into the street, but before he could take another, a movement on the other side caught the corner of his eye. When he turned his head toward it, he saw his father bolting out the door of the Connemara Gardens and rushing headlong toward the roadway. Without a thought, Billy sprang forward. The truck was by then so close that he could feel the heat of its engine. With the sound of a blasting horn assaulting his ears, he lunged forward, grabbed Leo, and tried to restrain him. With superior strength, Leo forced a pivot and pushed Billy back toward the sidewalk. He lost his balance, though, and fell forward, taking Billy down with him to the gutter, where they lay in their first embrace.

20 - Beholding

As Maggie drove down Columbia Road into her old neighborhood, a smattering of newly

refurbished three-deckers diverted her mind from the events of the last few hours, which had been roiling her mind like a circular nightmare. New siding in bright colors, big replacement windows, and roof decks exuded confidence that the neighborhood was on the rebound from years of neglect by absentee landlords, but they also made the faded, peeling houses surrounding them look slighted and sad, especially on a cloudy, dismal day like this one.

It was the latter perspective that pulled Maggie back to her plight: First, she had lost her mother through her own stupid negligence—letting her slip out of the house and disappear into a snow squall? Oh, and it turned out that she'd lost her son, too, although she didn't know it until Sister Esther called to tell her that Joe had "violated protocol" by "covertly" enlisting a friend to cover his route and that as a result, Robby had ended up in Dorchester. *Dorchester*? Then, after she had listened to her voicemail and called Wil to chew him out for *his* stupid negligence—bailing on their son to hunt down a ballplayer?—all she heard were low, muffled voices, as if the phone were still in a pocket or something. At that point, having apparently lost contact with her husband, she turned to chewing herself out for not calling him earlier, as if her grilling by the phantom bicycle hadn't already made her feel bad enough about that, but not worse than she felt about losing her mother. And so, the cycle repeated.

Desperate to break it, Maggie indulged in the fantasy that all this wasn't really happening.

"It *is* a nightmare," she whispered. "I'm just having a nightmare."

Reality didn't yield, though, and to make matters worse, the dark side of her Catholic upbringing—guilt and penance—asserted that God must be punishing her for some unspecified sin or inadequacy. Since her father's death, this thought had been like an infection that lay dormant and then raged during times of distress. Now, though, instead of letting the guilt plague her as she had when Robby and then Edna were diagnosed, Maggie lashed back at it.

"What have I ever done to deserve what's happened today? Nothing. *Nothing!* I've been good to Edna. I've been good to Robby. I've been good to Wil. I've even been good to his parents! And it hasn't always been easy. My mother was a bossy know-it-all, and now she's . . . she's . . . *senile*! My beautiful little boy lives in a bubble and my in-laws are condescending snobs! And my husband? He's a . . . a pushy know-it-all, just like my mother used to be! But, I repeat, *I've been good to them!* And you know why? *I love them!* That's supposed to be easy, but it's not. *They wear me out*! But I love them! I love them because . . . because . . . *I HAVE NO CHOICE!*"

By the end of her self-defense, Maggie was shouting. And, for the second time that day, crying. She pulled into the parking lot of Crispy Chicks Take Out, where she let the tears, now accompanied by heaving groans, have free rein. Truth be told, she strained to keep them going as long as she could because they were surprisingly comforting—even better than a bowl of soup. Soon they subsided, though, into sniffles, at which point she wiped her eyes with her fingertips and listened to her breathing as it steadied.

For a few minutes, Maggie watched people leave the restaurant carrying white bags and gallon buckets; some were already nibbling on legs or wings. She now remembered that this garish cement and glass building stood on the site of the long-since demolished Sheila Shanahan School of Dance, a cute little brick storefront where Maggie had learned—or tried to learn—tap, ballet, and Irish step back in third and fourth grades. It didn't matter how lame her shuffle-ball-change and arabesque and jig were, she still got to be in the recital in June at John Hancock Hall in downtown Boston, a real theater with dressing rooms and stage lights and curtains and rows and rows of seats. And even if she was a little out of sync with the rest of her group, everybody in the audience clapped and cheered. And afterwards, Sweety gave her flowers and brought her and Edna to Howard Johnson's or the Napoli. And when Edna got a little cross and said they should save their money and eat at home, he smiled and kissed her cheek and said, "Dearie, you're both worth the splurge."

Sweety. Sweety was easy to love.

"*But remember, Mags,*" she imagined him saying, "*you gotta love even when it is isn't easy.*"

Maggie nodded the way she used to whenever her father delivered his wisdom, and then she pulled back out onto Columbia Road. After the turn onto Dot Ave, she started checking for building numbers. As she approached a weathered little grocery at the corner of Russell Street, her face brightened.

"Oh, my God. It's Eddie's."

Maggie hadn't connected the address with the store where she had worked during high school, where her mother had worked before her and where, years later, Wil became a regular.

"Eddie is quintessential Dot, Maggie," he once told her, "even if he's not Irish. His accent alone is priceless. He actually said to me today, 'Ya wanna odda some con beef?' And the store?

My God, it's a set from a Frank Capra movie!"

Maggie's own memories of the place were warm, too, for it was Eddie who had helped her the most after Sweety's death. Unlike everybody else, he never offered condolences or reminisced about Sweety, all of which she didn't want and at least then, didn't need. And he never asked her how she was doing. Maggie was especially grateful to him for this because she didn't know how she was doing or how she felt, and trying to verbalize her loss, as she'd had to do at the wake and on her return to school, just made it feel heavier. Eddie seemed to get all this, so he just made sure she had plenty of work to do and bologna sandwiches to eat and avuncular hugs when her shifts were done.

Maggie parked a block down and was walking back toward the store when she saw a tow truck removing a silver-toned Suburban LT that was parked in a loading zone.

"That's all I'd need," she said, and hurried back to her own car to make sure that her space was legal.

When she finally reached Eddie's, she stopped to look at some old photos on display in the window. She shook her head at one of herself packing a bag with groceries, still dressed in her

Monsignor Farrell uniform. She remembered the day in ninth grade when Eddie had taken the picture. He kept prompting her to look up and smile, but as usual, she was too camera shy. Not so her mother, whose image Maggie spotted next, gorgeously beaming right at the lens as if the camera were her boyfriend.

"Dear God, Mum," she said to the photo. "Where are you? Where *are* you?"

As if in answer to the question, Maggie's phone rang. She didn't recognize the number on the screen, but she answered the call anyway because it could be someone with news about Edna.

"Hello?" she said hopefully.

But the voice that answered was Wil's.

"Maggie? Oh, thank God. Where have you been? I've been . . ."

Maggie felt a swell of anger, but she suppressed the urge to unleash it. She wanted Wil to see how she felt, not just to hear it. And she wanted to see him looking as guilty as she felt.

"I . . . I can't talk now, Wil," she said with a tone so brusque that she almost apologized for it. "I'm . . . I'm in the middle of something."

"But what . . ."

Maggie tapped the end-call icon, but within seconds, the phone rang again, a call from the same number. She stared at the words "Accept" and "Decline" at the bottom of the screen. Swallowing hard, she tapped the latter.

As soon as she entered the store, her turmoil dissipated. She was greeted by the same dark wainscoted walls, milky glass-globed ceiling lamps, narrow aisles of wooden shelving, and red soft-drink cooler that had always been here. There were the same canisters of candy and of pickled eggs on the counter and a clunky old cash register behind it, but still no lottery machine or rolls of scratch tickets hanging from the wall. ("Folks are poor enough," Eddie had once told her. "I'm not gonna encourage them to blow eighty bucks a week on a pipe dream.") Nothing had changed, at least here.

She looked for Eddie at his usual spot behind the meat case, but instead, she found him leaning against the floor-model ice-cream freezer in the far corner of the room, his head down and his shoulders slumped. Her heart instantly went out to him. He looked as if he were having as rough a day as she was.

"Hi, Eddie," Maggie said, sounding more cheerful than she felt.

He looked up and frowned, as if he didn't recognize her, but then he smiled. It was not his normal smile, though, the one that made his upper lip disappear and revealed a gold-capped tooth. This smile was muted and almost as sad as his posture.

"Miss Maggie," he said as he straightened up. "*Mirabile visu.*"

"Still watching *Jeopardy*, I see," she replied. "Let's see if I remember my Latin: *a wonderful sight*, right?"

He walked over to her with a bit of a limp she hadn't seen before and enveloped her in a hug,

during which she pressed back tears.

"You got it, kid. Now what brings you back to me?" he asked as their arms disengaged.

"Oh, your awesome personality, for one thing." She wanted to see his happy smile—she needed to see it—but all she got was another lukewarm grin.

"Irresistible, right?"

"You bet. And, well, I also hear you've been babysitting my son."

"Oh . . ."

If Maggie didn't know him so well, his tone would have worried her. It sounded . . . uneasy. But more likely, he was just as surprised as she was.

"So . . . so *you're* his mother?"

"Yeah. Crazy, huh? I guess Joe, the regular driver for Saint Theresa's, got his friend to do the route . . ."

"That's Billy—Billy Nee. He works for me here," Eddie interjected. "He was just trying to do Joe a favor."

"And the driver—I mean, Billy—brought Robby here because he didn't have our address, right? But why didn't he just call the school?"

"Because he knew if he did, Joe'd get canned, and . . ."

Maggie held up a hand. "Let me guess. He thought old, dependable Eddie would figure out a way to get Robby home *and* save Joe's job."

Eddie sighed. "Yeah, but, uh, I had to disappoint him. I mean, by tellin' him to call the cops."

When his face turned downcast again, Maggie held herself back from asking, "Is that why you look so sad?" He had always respected her privacy. She would respect his.

"What else could you do, Eddie? You didn't have any choice," Maggie offered. When Eddie made no response, she forced a smile and cheerful tone. "And look at it this way—at least Billy brought Robby someplace safe, my old hangout. How great is that?"

"Well . . ."

"Oh, come on. My little lost boy ending up here? It's like karma. Where is he, anyway? Oh, and Billy? I'd like to thank him."

"Ah . . . they're not here. I mean, right this minute."

"Where are they, then?" Now she sounded uneasy.

"They . . . went out. Just a coupla minutes ago. But, uh, they should be back soon."

"Oh . . . well, I guess if Billy's kept Robby safe this long, I don't have to worry, right? He must be a good guy—Billy, I mean, y'know, to care so much about Joe, and to be so close to you, of course."

"Billy's an ace. He just doesn't know it. His old man pretty much demoed his self-confidence."

"Billy Nee," Maggie said. "Why does that name sound familiar? Would I know him from Saint A's, maybe?"

"Prob'ly not. He was just a squirt when you were in high school. But he did a paper route on your street, I think."

"That's it! Oh, he was a cute little kid and nice, too. I remember one Christmas when Sweety made him cookies, and the next day, Billy delivered a homemade thank-you card with the newspaper."

"Yup. That'd be Billy."

"But his father?"

"Was a major league asshole. Still is."

"That's too bad. But at least Billy's got you, Eddie."

"Yeah, well, for better or for worse."

They fell into silence, but not the comfortable kind that used to happen when they were stocking shelves or cleaning up. After their eyes met, looking up at the clock on the wall,

Maggie made an attempt at conversation at the same moment that Eddie did.

"The place looks . . ." Maggie started to say.

"How's your . . ." Eddie began and then, nodding, said, "You first."

"I was going to say that the place looks . . . good, Eddie. Just like home."

"Yeah, if home's the poorhouse. Billy gets on me to modernize, but I've always said if it ain't broke, don't fix it, and . . ."

"If it is broke, make do," Maggie said, with a giggle. "Yes, you have always said that."

"You know, I think it was your mother who came up with that line. It was her way of razzing me. God, she was a hot sketch. Say, how is she, anyway—and Wil? That's what I was gonna ask you."

"Oh, they're . . ."

Maggie was about to tell him everything that had happened on that nightmare day: the snow blowing in through the open front door, Officer Preston's scary eyebrows, the bicycle-skeleton's insinuations, the meltdown at Crispy Chicks, and the phone call she spitefully declined. Eddie wouldn't tell her not to worry. He wouldn't assure her that her mother was all right or that her husband deserved the chance to explain himself. But he wouldn't disappoint her, either. Because he would listen, and his heart would go out to her the same way hers went out to him just a few minutes earlier when she saw him looking so sad. And then the weight of everything that had been pressing down on her so relentlessly wouldn't be quite as heavy because he would bear it with her.

Maggie didn't say anything, though, because at that moment Eddie's head turned toward the door, and she heard him repeat, in an astonished tone, what he had said to her when she walked in.

"*Mirabile visu.*"

21 - Mission: Eddie Jack's

When Billy opened his eyes, he found himself lying flat on his back with his prostrate father on top of him. He wasn't sure how long they had been there, but he did remember what he'd done, and he knew that it worked because he heard and smelled Leo's heaving, beery breath. He couldn't see the old man's face, though, because the two of them were literally cheek-to-jowl. As if this weren't weird enough, above them, someone drifted into Billy's focus, Eamon Lally, the missing Red Sox player?

At that point, Billy closed his eyes and after a few steadying breaths, reopened them, hoping to see something reasonable appear this time. Granted, a few minutes earlier, he had started to enact his old run-in-front-of-a-truck daydream, which he'd never before had the balls to do, and then he ended up saving his father from doing the very thing Billy used to hope the bastard would do, knowing he'd never be that accommodating, and now they were lying in a gutter on Dot Ave. So, really, what kind of *reasonable* was he expecting to see? He wasn't sure about this either, just not a major league baseball player hovering over them. But when he took another look, Lally's face was still there, even closer.

"Man, you really are lost," Billy said to what he was sure was a posttraumatic vision.

"Used to be," the vision said. "But I found myself."

Billy was about to close his eyes again because having a conversation with someone who couldn't possibly be there was kind of freaking him out. Then he spotted someone else standing nearby—the kid from the van. He was flanked by an old lady and a priest, a trio which was almost as weird as the Red Sox guy, but now Billy kept his eyes open because he was not going to lose this kid again, even in a hallucination.

"Okay, now, I'm just going to gently roll you off, sir," Eamon said, kneeling over Leo. "Nice and easy on three—one, two, three."

Once separated, father and son both lay on their backs, side by side, like two disheveled, misplaced stargazers.

"The fuck you do that for?" Leo moaned.

"Well, sir," Eamon answered, "I thought you'd be more comfortable, and my mother—she's a Red Cross nurse—taught me . . ."

"He's talking to me," Billy said as reality dawned, and to Leo, he was about to say, "Beats the hell outta me," when Mum in his head spoke up.

"*You did a good thing, Billy. Don't spoil it now.*"

So, he coughed and replied, "I don't know. Some kind of instinct, I guess."

As relieved as Billy was to hear his mother's voice again, the truth was that he wasn't concerned with her advice or with his father's condition or with the apparent fact that a Cy Young winner was ministering to them. The only thing on his mind was getting the kid, who, thank God, was still looking on, back to the store and his mother before she reported a kidnapping.

Grimacing, he worked his way to his feet. He was sore and unsteady, but even being bullet ridden wouldn't have kept him from completing this little episode of *Mission: Impossible* he'd been stuck in half the day. He stepped toward the sidewalk and held his hand out to the kid, who looked at him with his shepherd-boy eyes and accepted it.

"Let's go see your mum, buddy."

Eamon said, "Whoa, man! You'd better take it easy until the paramedics get here and check you out. They're on their way."

Billy glared at him.

"No, no, no, no. I am this kid's driver. I am supposed to get him to his mother. I am *going* to get him to his mother," he replied with the fervor of a squadron leader in combat. For emphasis, he pointed his outstretched arm up the avenue and asserted, "She's waiting for him at the corner store down the street. That's where I am going to bring him. Now."

"Eddie Jack's?" Edna piped up. "Why, I'm going there, too! I've got to get some corned beef for Sweety's supper. Maybe we can all go together—you, me, and Robby!"

She took the boy's free hand and turned toward Monsignor Canny.

"Would you like to go too, Father? It's the best corned beef in the city—the gray kind."

"Wait," Billy said to Edna, "Sweety? Sweety McDonough? But he's. . . . Are you . . . ? Is this kid your . . . ?"

"He's my . . . very special friend," Edna replied brightly, "just like the man down there on the ground."

His mouth hanging open, Billy looked first at Leo, who smiled dreamily and said, “She was my first la . . . lady,” and then to Edna who claimed, “I was a wild ride, you know.”

Finally, Billy turned to the priest, his eyes imploring him to make some sense of this madness.

“Well, I don’t know about all that,” Monsignor Canny said in the even tone of someone who heard it all for a living, “but they were sitting together inside the bar, with the little boy. I noticed them when Eamon and I were talking.”

Billy nodded, as he assessed the situation: *Okay, so the little space cadet slipped out of Eddie’s and ended up in a bar with my father and his old girlfriend, who wants to make supper for a dead guy and may be the kid’s grandma or something, and a priest and a missing ballplayer were having a beer. Does not matter. I’m. Still. Getting. The. Kid. Back. To. The. Store.*

Before Billy could set out, though, Monsignor Canny took hold of his arm.

“I’d better go with you . . . I’m sorry, what’s your name?”

“Billy,” Leo answered from below. “He’s my kid.”

“Billy,” the priest repeated, without so much as a raised eyebrow. “For safety’s sake, Billy, let me come along. You’re obviously shaken, and the lady here needs a reliable companion. Eamon can stay with the gentleman, I mean, your father and go . . .”

Leo’s voice rose again.

“I’m Leo. And believe me, Father, I’m no gentleman, sad to say.”

The priest smiled at him and continued addressing Eamon. “And go along with Leo to the hospital if paramedics take him in before I get back from accompanying you and Edna to the store.”

"And Robby, Father," Edna reminded him. "Don't forget Robby."

"Forgive me, Edna. And Robby, of course."

"Sure thing, Monsignor," Eamon replied, "and we can catch up later at the seminary, so I can, y'know, find out about signing on."

Billy had been looking up the street toward the store, on the lookout for a squad car, but when he heard this, his head pivoted.

"Jeez, man, *that's* where you found yourself?" he asked.

Eamon nodded, radiating the joy of self-discovery, just like Joe's and Drew's voices had earlier. Envy resurged in Billy's throat. How the hell many people were going to rub his nose in their freakin' happiness and contentment today? The closest he felt to either was that he no longer had the urge to make contact with an oncoming ton-and-a-half motor vehicle.

After clearing his throat, he said, "Cool. Yeah. Whatever."

"*Good enough, Billy. Now say something nice to your father.*"

"Ah, Mum . . . I mean, ah . . . Leo, I'll get over to the hospital after I finish what I have to do."

"*A little more . . .*" Mum in his head urged.

"Hang in, okay?"

"Ya didn't give much goddamn choice, did ya?" Leo grumbled.

For a moment, they caught each other's eyes, and with a reflex conditioned over the years, they immediately averted them. Whatever it was they saw in that moment, though, brought them back for another look, and this produced for each a slim and begrudging, but undeniable, rise of the cheeks.

And then, hand-in-hand, the unlikely quartet headed up the avenue to Eddie Jack's.

22 - The Old Stomping Ground

Charlie Costello pulled into the space next to Wil's car in the Saint Francis Seminary parking lot. Turning his expansive girth and plump, rosy, face toward his passenger, he said, "Thanks again, Wil, for taking care of Rita."

"Glad to help, Charlie. I just hope it's what they think it is."

"Oh, it's a panic attack, all right. Classic Rita. Her head gets all worked up over something, and then her body gets into the act, and then her head gets even more worked up. I can never calm her down, so I just bring her to the hospital, and they keep her overnight. They say it's for observation; I say it's for ass-covering. Then they adjust her medication and send her on her way. Thank God I got good insurance."

"Yeah, well, thank you for the ride, Charlie."

As Wil stepped out of the car, Charlie called out, "Hey, Wil, what do you say we go for a beer as long as we're here in our old stomping ground? I haven't been back to the Connemara in years. I remember they used to have the best Guinness around."

Part of Wil wanted to get home and see what the hell Maggie was in the middle of that made her sound so strange on the phone. It occurred to him that she might be pissed that he canceled on Robby, but whenever he'd done it before, she came across as disappointed and hurt, not cold and dismissive. As anxious as he was to find out what was going on, another part of him wanted to put it off, hoping that if he did, she'd be back to normal by the time he got home. A couple of beers would kill some time—and God knew he deserved them—but Wil didn't want to risk seeing Eamon Lally and Monsignor Canny again.

"Make it the Bantry, Charlie, and you've got a deal."

"Oooh. Down and dirty—you are an old Dot rat. I like it. Hey, the snow let up, so let's walk. I'll show you where my daughter lives, and with any luck, I'll find Rita's car."

As they walked down Dot Ave, Charlie scanned the motley three-deckers and low-end storefronts—a sub shop, a discount store, an insurance agency, a beauty parlor—smiling like an enraptured tourist on the Paseo del Prado.

"This is gonna sound weird," he said, "but I miss Dorchester. Oh, I know, Chestnut Hill's nice—fabulous, really—but I grew up here, you know? It's still home, in a way. Rita's from here, too; she lived just across Madison Green Street from my house."

"High school sweethearts?" Wil asked.

"First grade at Saint A's. I made her a special valentine with hearts and glitter and all, and on the inside, I wrote, 'To the prettiest girl in first grade.' I misspelled every word, but she gave me a kiss for it anyway."

"Impressive."

"What can I say? I had skills."

"Why did you leave, Charlie? Dot, I mean. If you liked it so much."

"Oh, when I got promoted to VP, Rita thought it'd look better if we lived some place fancier. I think *appropriate* is the word she used. It seemed kind of stuck up to me, but y'know,

'If mama ain't happy, ain't nobody happy,' so I went along with it."

As Wil recalled the similar logic he had used with Maggie, his right eyelid twitched.

Charlie pointed to a large, gray stucco building that Wil knew was once a protestant church before the Irish Catholic influx more than a century ago. By the time he lived here with Maggie, it had long since become a community center.

"I used to play basketball there in fifth and sixth grade—seventh, too, maybe. Sweety McDonough was my coach, y'know."

"Maggie's dad? Really?"

"Oh, yeah. Great guy, *great* guy. Probably not the best coach, to be honest with you, but we didn't care. He was like a . . . a young uncle who just gets you in a way your father doesn't—y'know what I'm sayin'? And it wasn't some phony, put-on thing just to make us like him. He was the real deal. We like owned the bottom of the league, but, man, we loved to play because . . . well, this sounds corny, but we loved him."

The twinge recurred, repeating itself three or four times, and Wil rubbed his eyelid.

"And I tell ya, when I found out he got killed . . ."

Charlie swallowed hard, and his happy face constricted.

"It was a blow. I mean, I hadn't seen him for a long while, but the memories . . . I wasn't the only one who felt that way, either. Five other guys from the team got together with me to set up a memorial fund in his name for the community center. He deserved it, too. I mean, he was so good to us that we just wanted to keep that part of him alive."

Wil had heard a lot of stories about Sweety from Edna, mostly since she'd been in her current state—his acts of kindness, his sympathetic ear, his self-effacing nature—all told in the present tense, as if she were expecting him to come home any minute, which Wil suspected she was. Maggie, on the other hand, spoke of him only occasionally, and whenever she did, her voice quavered. Wil had never been able to understand how her sadness could be so fresh after such a long time. Sure, it could have something to do with the way the poor guy died, but still, it was over twenty years ago. Now, listening to Charlie, Wil remembered how choked up he himself got at Peg Joyce's funeral last year, even though he had known her kindness for only a few months.

"And you and Maggie, Wil," Charlie said, stopping short to look Wil straight in the eye. "You're like a whole other memorial to Sweety, even though I know you yourself never met him. Taking care of Edna and your son—Robby, right?—when a lot of other people would have let somebody else do it. It's just the kind of thing Sweety would have done. And then you looked out for Rita today when you must have had a million things to do."

He enveloped Wil in a big-cherub hug, like the one he'd gotten from Lovie Joyce, Tommy's father, when he bumped into him at Fenway last fall.

"Bless you, Wil. Bless you."

By the time Charlie disengaged, Wil's eye was twitching so much that he felt as if he were winking. He didn't want

Charlie's blessing, because he hadn't earned it. He was *not* a memorial to Sweety. He was practically the guy's antithesis—cocky, self-centered, manipulative. Suddenly confession enticed Wil for the second time that day. Come clean to Charlie. The thought was *so* Saint Frank, and yet Wil was drawn to it. He could tell this sweet, sentimental, stand-up guy about duping Eamon and bailing on Robby and trying to dump Rita on a stranger. Maggie had often told him how good she felt after going to confession, although he could never imagine what the hell she had to confess. Maybe it would work for him, too. Okay, Charlie Costello wasn't a priest, but he was at least a Catholic and a good person. The concept was the same, so maybe the effect would be, too. Or . . . Wil could go back to the Connemara after all and tell Monsignor Canny and Eamon the truth about himself. That would be harder, but maybe it would enhance the relief.

Before Wil had time to dismiss either notion, Charlie composed himself and was talking again.

"Hey, look, Wil! Eddie Jack's is just across the street. There was another great guy, I tell ya.

Sweety used to bring us in there after games for sodas, and Eddie'd give us free penny candy. I wonder if he's still working."

"He was when we left. You know, I liked him, too."

"Whaddya say we make a quick stop and say hi?" Charlie suggested.

Wil didn't know if he was relieved or disappointed to be diverted from confession, but the idea of finding Eddie behind the meat case just like old times appealed to him.

"Why not? I mean, we're back in our old stomping ground, right?"

"Ha! There ya go!" Charlie exclaimed.

Epilogue - A Year Later

After her ESL class, Maggie walks upstairs to the adult daycare room, where she finds Edna stirring a pot of soup on an island stovetop under the watchful eye of Eamon Lally, now a seminarian doing community service. Other volunteers direct their elders in slicing bread, pouring juice, and setting the table.

"Cream of potato has always been my mum's favorite," Eamon says to Edna.

Her eyes fixed on the task at hand, she replies, "I used to know your mum, y'know."

"You did, did you?"

She looks around, as if challenged to find proof, and when her eyes alight on Maggie, exclaims, "Why, look! Here she is now!"

"What's cooking, guys?" Maggie asks, as she approaches.

Edna's voice rings out, "Soup!"

"Oh, I love soup. What kind?"

Edna looks down at the pot.

"Um . . . white!"

"I like that the best!" Maggie effuses, a hand splayed on her chest.

"Me too!"

Edna turns to Eamon and asks, "Can your mum stay for lunch?"

"Edna, there's always room at our table for one more. We'll put her right next to you," he replies, tossing Maggie a wink.

Once seated, Edna looks at Maggie and frowns.

"I'm sorry, dear, but I can't remember your name."

"Maggie."

"Oh, yes. Maggie."

Edna sips her soup and nods.

"Maggie's a good girl. She brought me home."

♦ ♦ ♦

Later that afternoon, Maggie and Edna sit in wicker rockers on the porch of a once gracious but now in-recovery Victorian on Mellon Street, a few blocks from the community center. The towering maple tree in the front yard is still bare and the small patch of grass is barely green, but the sun is delivering the warmth of May, and a few crocuses Maggie planted back in October are peeking up along the walkway.

Last year, a few weeks after everyone she loved and a few she would come to love converged on Eddie Jack's, where they all found more than what they were looking for, she suggested to Wil that they move back to Dorchester.

"I know Chestnut Hill's . . . fabulous and everything, and Dorchester's, well, not, but I grew up there. It's still home, in a way and I . . . I miss it," she said and then braced herself when she saw the wry smile that was usually Wil's prelude to a rebuttal. That time, though, she read the smile wrong.

"Yeah," he replied quietly. "That feels . . . appropriate."

Now, as she and Edna are enjoying their first afternoon outside since the fall, Edna says, "Robby's coming soon, right?"

"Yes, he is, Mum," Maggie replies, reaching over to squeeze her arm. "You remembered."

"Oh, I always remember Robby."

"Yeah, you do. You always remember Robby."

Before Edna has a chance to repeat herself, a Chevy Cavalier that does not show its age pulls up in front of the house. Maggie takes Edna's hand, and they walk together to the curb, where Billy Nee is waiting for them.

"Hey, Billy," Maggie says.

"Hey, Maggie. Hey, Edna."

"Hi, handsome," Edna drawls as she must have in her wild-ride days. "Don't I know you from somewhere?"

After similar encounters over the past six months, Billy is used to being hit on by a woman in her seventies who thinks she is in her twenties.

"Oh, come on, Edna. Don't tell me you forgot."

Her eyes lit up.

"Physical activity?"

"Um, not the kind you're thinking of, Edna."

"Mum," Maggie interjects. "Billy's an aide at Robby's school, and he drives him home, remember?"

"Oh, yes," replies Edna in a disappointed tone that quickly perks up.

"Where *is* Robby?"

Billy opens the car door, and Robby pops out.

"Mum-ma," he says in a soft, musical tone. "Nan-a, Bil-ly."

He sings this tune-of-sorts as randomly as a baby babbles, and like a new mother's, Maggie's heart sings along with every syllable of it.

"Would you like to sit and rock with Nana, Robby?" Edna asks, holding out her hand.

"Mum-ma, Nan-a, Bil-ly," he sings as the two repair to the porch.

"Music therapy's done so much for him," Maggie says to Billy. "Thank God Charlie suggested Bridget do her internship at Saint T's."

"Yeah, I'm pretty psyched about that, too."

Maggie shoots him a teasing smile and says, "Especially since she dumped the graffiti guy and took up with a certain UMass student."

"It's added to her appeal, yeah," Billy replies. "I mean, good taste counts."

"And obviously, she has it. But hey, speaking of UMass Boston, how's cognitive science going?" Maggie asks.

"Pretty well. I mean, sometimes I feel like it's feeding my brain and other times like it's eating it."

Maggie nods.

"Education's weird like that."

"I guess so. And none of it would be happening if you and Wil hadn't gotten me to apply and then convinced Sister Esther to hire me so I could afford it."

"Ah, I get it. Cognitive science, Sister Esther. We're a mixed blessing."

"Only on the days when I feel like I should go back to stocking Eddie's shelves."

"Oh, forget that idea, buddy. Eddie would tell you to tough it out. He believes you're going to make it, and so do we."

Billy looks away, as he always does when someone gives him a compliment.

"You sound like Bridget."

"See? You're outnumbered."

"Looks like it," Billy says. "Y'know, even Leo's on your side. Of course, he phrased it differently."

"How so?"

Mimicking his father's gravelly baritone, Billy growls, "No way you're fuckin' up this chance, kid."

Maggie laughs and says, "I love it! Say, I saw Leo the other day at Eddie's. He looks really good. I guess working for the monsignor agrees with him?"

"Yeah, it's hard to believe. I mean, he's done maintenance before, but he always got fired for drinking on the job or calling the boss a prick or . . . well, it's a long, pathetic list."

"What do you think is making the difference this time?"

"I don't know. It could be because he likes the monsignor, and Eamon, too. After that time last year when he got hurt and they helped him, he kind of bonded with them. Or it could just be that all the paintings and statues of saints scare him into submission."

"Or," Maggie says slowly, "it could be that he's grateful to his son for saving his life and he wants to do right by him."

"Yeah, well . . . whatever."

Billy looks up the street, just as Wil's car turns onto it.

"Looks like your husband's home."

Wil parks his SUV behind Billy's car, walks to the cargo bed, and pulls out a long box.

"You got it!" Maggie calls out.

When Wil reaches them, he pats Billy's shoulder and gives Maggie a kiss.

"It's just the basic model, but it should be fine for our purpose."

"A keyboard?" Billy asks, looking at the box.

"Yeah, it's for Robby," Wil says. "I noticed he likes to play on the piano at the community

Center, so we figured this might encourage his interest."

"And maybe help his speech, too," Maggie adds.

As if on cue, Robby sings out from the porch, "Dad-da, Mum-ma, Bil-ly, Nan-a."

His face as radiant as if he has just been called up to receive the Pulitzer, Wil says goodbye to Billy and hurries toward his son.

"Can you stay for dinner, Billy," Maggie asks, "and maybe a concert? We're having corned beef."

"Hey, I'd love to, but I'm presenting my term paper in class tonight, and I've got to practice some more. I'll tell Bridget about the keyboard, though, when I see her later. She'll be psyched."

"I think so, too," Maggie says.

When he is behind the wheel again, she sticks her head into the passenger side window and says, "Hey, if I don't see you in the morning, I'll put some corned beef sandwiches in Robby's backpack for you and Bridget."

"Awesome. Thanks, Maggie."

♦ ♦ ♦

"Here I go, Mum," Billy says as he drives off. "Big night. And you'll be happy to know I've got some serious positive energy going."

He grins, even though he's gotten no reply. In fact, Billy has not heard his mother's voice in over six months. Her silence troubled him for a while because he couldn't figure out what he had done to cause it. One night, he admitted his concern to Eamon over beers at the Connemara.

"So, like, what do you think's going on?" Billy asked.

"Well, I don't know for sure, Billy," Eamon said, "but it could be that now that you've found a career path and a nice girlfriend and all, your mum's finally . . . well, resting in peace."

He picked up his bottle and took a swig.

"But I bet ya anything, she'll still be listening if you talk to her."

So, Billy started doing just that, usually at the end of the day or when he was alone in the car. At first, he reported to her daily on his hopes, mostly that he would not screw up his relationship with Bridget or his chance to get a degree, but over time, the briefings have become more upbeat as some fledgling self-confidence crept into them. As it did, the updates became shorter and less frequent, although Billy hasn't noticed.

♦ ♦ ♦

Like Billy, Maggie no longer hears from the other side, but she is comfortable with the change because after her last Sweety Dream on the night Robby and Edna were found, she finally understood the message her father had tried to give her the week before her wedding, something that she subsequently learned on her own.

As the more recent dream started, she and Wil, in their wedding attire, were sitting at the head of a table draped with a white linen cloth and set with gleaming china and silverware.

Around it were gathered Edna, Robby, Eddie Jack, Billy, Leo, Joe, Charlie, Bridget, Monsignor Canny, and Eamon. Diego Ortega entered, wearing a tuxedo with a greengrocer's apron over it, and carrying a silver serving platter with a dome cover, which he placed in front of Maggie and Wil. With a flourish, he removed the lid, revealing a large mound of celery hearts, one of which he picked up. After the platter had been passed around, Ortega raised his stalk and calls out, "A toast!"

Everyone followed suit, their faces glowing in the candlelight.

"To having no choice!" Ortega said, as he smiled down at Maggie and Wil.

"To having no choice!" the diners echoed.

And then they feasted.

Thank you so much for reading *The Right Place at the Right Time.* If you've enjoyed the book, we would be grateful if you would post a review on the bookseller's website.

Just a few words is all it takes!

Acknowledgments

Thanks to my English-teacher friends, Dan Farber, Sharon Hamilton, Roger Stacey, Bonnie Pooley, Mac Davis, Darcy Chase and Brian Staveley for their thoughtful suggestions on my first draft. I hope I've earned a good final grade.

Thanks also to Sheri Williams and her staff at TouchPoint Press for accepting the manuscript and affirming my hope that you're never too old to give it a shot, and to my editor, Kelly Esparza, for patiently guiding me through my technological confusion. Thank you to Bill Forry for permission to use the photo of the Dorchester Market. Most of all, thanks to my husband and best friend, Bob O'Brien, for his love and support.

Printed in the USA
CPSIA information can be obtained
at www.ICGtesting.com
CBHW011142170824
13314CB00013B/237